*Captured by a band of thieves,
how will Diego escape?*

Diego waited awhile to be sure Weasel was asleep again. Then he leaned out the window as far as he could without jumping....Below the window, he saw the steep slope of the roof. At its base, it touched a wall embedded with jagged iron spikes.

No one, Diego thought, *could climb over that wall, but someone small might find a way to get through those spikes. Down and off and free!*

He smiled. "Come the dawn, I'll find a way somehow."

Diego Columbus
Adventures on the High Seas

Marni McGee

illustrations by Jim Hsieh

Fleming H. Revell Company
Tarrytown, New York

For Sears
husband, historian, critic,
and friend

Text copyright © 1992 by Marni McGee

Art copyright © 1992 by March Media, Inc.

Book development by March Media, Inc.

Published by the Fleming H. Revell Company

Tarrytown, New York 10591

Printed in the United States of America

ISBN 0-8007-5433-6

Contents

Chapter I

The Queen Commands

*D*iego kicked his heels against the leathery flanks of the mule. "Come on, Loca. Move!"

Riding beside him was Christopher Columbus, his long legs almost touching the ground. "Is the mule too slow for you, son?"

"She's as stubborn as the Queen," Diego complained. "We should change her name to Isabella, queen of mules."

The third rider spoke. "Young man, you are speaking of Her Royal Highness, the Queen of Spain. Queen of mules, indeed! That tongue of yours will get you in trouble someday."

"You're right to scold, Friar Juan," Christopher said, "but the Queen has wronged me, and Diego feels the slight." His voice filled with sudden anger. "For six long years, she kept me waiting — dangling on her royal hook. And for what? Now it has all come to nothing."

"Even though she promised," Diego insisted. "She promised that after the war with Granada . . ."

Christopher shrugged. "Perhaps I was foolish to be so trusting. I had nothing in writing."

"She gave you her word. Doesn't a queen have to keep her word? Doesn't God judge her like anyone else?"

"Perhaps you should ask Friar Juan that question."

"There are no easy answers," murmured the priest.

Pushing a lock of curly brown hair from his face, Diego faced him. "I remember, when I was little, I used to crawl up in Father's lap and listen to him talk. He'd tell me about his dream — sailing west to the Indies. Even then, I knew that someday he would do it. He wasn't afraid of whirlpools or monsters rising out of the sea." He turned to his father. "Somehow, as I grew, *your* dream became mine."

Christopher reached out and touched Diego's cheek. "I became a beggar for that dream, Diego, set adrift from home and from you. When your mother lay sick and dying, I didn't even know. I was off in Portugal, begging King John for ships. I didn't know."

"You mustn't blame yourself," Friar Juan said, fingering the cross that hung from his neck. "A man must always do what he believes is right."

Diego studied his father's face. "You won't give up, will you?"

"Give up?" Christopher roared. "Never! But I'll wait no more for the Queen. My mind is made up. I'll go to France. King Charles is willing to receive me. He's young and adventurous. He will gladly give me ships and men. *He* will see the promise of wealth and glory for France."

"And I shall go with you," Diego declared.

"You, Diego? No."

"I'm not a baby, Father. I'm twelve years old."

"You talk enough for *three* boys, Diego, but the fact is, you're small for your age. You've always been sickly, and this could be a difficult voyage."

"I could —"

Christopher shook his head. "No, my Diego! We'll spend the night at Piños-Puente, and tomorrow you will go with Friar Juan to La Rábida, back to the monastery. You'll be safe there."

"I don't *want* to be safe. I spent the last five years being safe at La Rábida, but now I should be with you. Ask Friar Juan. He understands."

"The boy may well be right," the priest agreed.

Christopher Columbus stuck out his jaw and said nothing. Beside him rode Diego. His forehead was wrinkled in a frown, and his chin was set just like his father's.

Friar Juan looked from one to the other. "There are more than three mules on the road to Piños-Puente," he chuckled.

Just then, Diego heard hoofbeats thudding toward them. "Someone's coming," he cried as he jumped to the ground and pulled his mule to the side of the path.

Galloping toward them was a huge black horse, its bridle glinting in the sun. The rider carried the banner of the Queen. As he drew near, he reined in his steed.

"I've come with a message for Christopher Columbus," he said. "Has he passed this way?"

"He's right here," Diego said, pointing to his father.

Christopher swung down from his mule's back. "I am the man you seek."

"Sir," said the messenger, "Her Royal Majesty asks that you return to the court."

"The Queen?" Diego gasped.

"Return?" Christopher stammered. "Now?"

"The arrangements have all been made," said the messenger. "You will stay the night with the royal treasurer, Señor Luis de Santángel. The Queen will receive you tomorrow."

Christopher bowed. "Please tell Her Majesty that I shall await her pleasure at court tomorrow."

The travelers watched as the messenger turned, waving one hand in salute. As he rode away, his woolen cape floated out behind him, fluttering in the chill wind.

Diego was the first to speak. "What does that woman think you are? A puppet on a string?"

Christopher slapped his knee. "That *woman*, as you call her, is one of the most powerful creatures on earth. A queen can change her mind as often as she changes her gown. We have no choice when a queen commands."

Diego's eyes sparkled. "*We*, Father?"

"Yes, Diego, I've decided to take you with me to see the Queen. Tomorrow you will meet Her Royal, Most Changeable Majesty — Isabella, Queen of Spain."

Chapter 2

Ready & Waiting

*D*iego sat in the Presence Chamber with his father, waiting to see the Queen. The guard at the door stood stiff and stern. Diego watched to see if he would smile or blink, but the guard did not move and his hand never left the hilt of his sword.

The room was large and square, lined with high-backed chairs. Its only light came from tall, narrow windows. Like huge, brightly colored rugs, tapestries covered the walls. Woven into each one, stitch by stitch, were scenes from ancient tales. The one that Diego liked best showed a shipwrecked sailor coming ashore in a storm, his battered ship in the distance.

Diego pointed it out. "Look at the one in the middle, Father. That could be *you*, when your ship was wrecked and you had to swim to shore."

Christopher chuckled. "You think I'm one of the heroes like Aeneas?"

"You will be, Father. Soon."

"I wish the Queen thought so."

Suddenly, Diego jumped up, hopping from one foot to the other. "What could she be doing all this time?"

"Queenly business," Christopher replied. "Stand still, Diego."

"I can't," Diego complained. "It's these clothes! The collar's choking me, and this shirt feels like a patch of briars."

"You look like a proper gentleman. At least you *would* if you weren't wiggling so. I just hope you won't fidget and scratch when we get to the Throne Room."

"I won't," Diego promised. "I remember what you said I must do — bow, stand still, and keep quiet. I practiced bowing this morning with Senor Santángel."

"Good," said his father, "and here he comes now."

"I'm sorry you had such a long wait," said Luis de Santángel as he rushed across the room.

"No matter," Christopher replied. "One expects to wait for a queen."

"Especially this one, eh?" said Santángel. He turned to Diego. "Are you ready to meet Her Royal Majesty, Queen Isabella of Spain?"

"More than ready, sir."

"Come along then."

The two men strode down the hallway side by side. Diego almost ran to keep up with them.

Señor Santángel took Christopher's arm. "I spoke with Her Majesty this morning. There's a good, strong wind at your back, my friend."

"It's hard to believe what has happened," Christopher said. "Not twenty-four hours ago, I left this place, rejected. But now, once again, there's hope. What did you *say* to change her mind?"

Santángel laughed. "Mainly, I appealed to her pride — I said I couldn't believe that she might let such an opportunity pass... that she would let another monarch reap the glory of this great discovery. 'While others trudge over land,' I said, 'we could be sailing home — our ships heavily loaded with spices and gold.' I made sure she knew that you had received an invitation from the King of France to come and talk about your great enterprise of the Indies."

"You're a powerful man, Santángel."

Luis de Santángel shook his head. "You are the one who is powerful. Yours was the vision, the plan. And you are the one who will face the unknown."

"Yes," Diego whispered. "And *I* will be at his side."

Christopher turned to his son. "What did you say?"

Diego grinned. "Nothing, Father, nothing!"

Chapter 3

The Queen Smiles

*A*t the door of the Throne Room, Señor Santángel spoke to the soldiers who stood guard. "Christopher Columbus and his son Diego await the Queen's pleasure."

The two guards stepped aside, stamping sharply with their boots. Huge doors swung open. Diego blinked. Torches lined the walls, and in the center was a throne that seemed itself to be made of light. On it sat the Queen. Her hair was red, like his father's, and her skin was as white as the clouds at summer's end. At her neck was a stiff white ruff. She wore a dark green velvet gown and on her fingers — so many rings!

Diego stared. His mouth was dry.

"Kneel," his father whispered as he dropped to one knee.

Diego dropped down beside his father and bowed his head.

The Queen spoke in ringing tones. "Christopher Columbus," she said, "I welcome you to the court of Spain. Rise and approach the throne."

Walking behind his father, Diego prayed he wouldn't trip.

The Queen's voice was rich and clear. "We are glad that you have returned. After much consideration, we are willing to speak once again about your enterprise of the Indies."

"At your service, Your Majesty. May I present my son, Diego Columbus?"

"Indeed. Come forward, young man. I cannot see you behind your father's girth."

Diego stepped out from his father's shadow. His heart thumped like a rabbit in a trap. "Your Majesty!"

"Don't be afraid of me," the Queen said with a smile. "I am known to be stern, but I, too, have children — a son not much older than you. Diego, do you know about your father's grand scheme and what he asks of Spain?"

"Yes, Your Majesty. My father knows all about maps and charts and tides."

The Queen nodded. Then she spoke to Christopher. "What troubles me most is the crew. Many fear to sail beyond the sight of land. You propose to sail uncharted seas."

"Your Majesty," Diego blurted out, "we can teach the men. It's only superstition that makes them so afraid."

"Diego!" Christopher exclaimed.

Isabella silenced him with a look. "*You* will teach the men, Diego? What makes you think that grown-up sailors will listen to a child?"

Diego's cheeks flushed hot, and he could feel his father's gaze burning into the back of his neck. "Because, Your Majesty, I'm going to sail with my father, and when people see that the Admiral's own son is going, they'll know there's nothing to fear."

"Diego, hush," Columbus commanded. "Your Majesty, forgive my son's outburst. He's not going — "

"There is nothing to forgive," the Queen replied.

Christopher sighed. "About the crew, Madam . . . I know, for a fact, that the port town of Palos is full of men who are eager to sail. They need the work if they are to feed their families. I'm certain I can gather a crew."

"Perhaps," said the Queen. She turned again to Diego. "Are you completely fearless, young man?"

"Yes . . . I mean, no, Your Highness," Diego stammered, "but it's not the sea that frightens me. And I'm never afraid with my father."

"Señor Santángel told me your mother is no longer alive."

"No, Your Highness, she died when I was five, and then, while Father was away, I lived in the monastery with Friar Juan."

"At La Rábida?"

Diego nodded.

"Ah, then you know how to read and write. Good." Queen Isabella held out her hands. "Come here."

Diego walked up the steps to the throne, drawn to the Queen like a piece of iron to a magnet. When she took his hands in hers, Diego caught his breath. He had never felt anything so soft and smooth as the Queen's white hands.

"I like your spirit, Diego. From this day forth, you are no longer a motherless boy. You have a mother in me. And in a few years, I will summon you to live at court."

"Yes, Your Majesty," Diego murmured as if in a dream.

"My family is honored," Christopher said, dropping again to one knee.

The Queen gently squeezed Diego's hands, then let them go. She motioned for Christopher to stand. "Now we can see why you insisted on being given a title — to be passed on to your children and to your children's children."

"For them, Your Majesty, but also for God and for Spain."

"We understand you," the Queen said kindly. "The waiting time is over at last."

"May God be praised," Christopher breathed.

With a nod, the Queen continued. "We have decided to provide three ships for your voyage. You shall be Admiral, Viceroy, and Governor in and over all the islands and mainlands that shall be discovered through your industry and labor. And you are now empowered, from this day forth, to call yourself *Sir* Christopher Columbus, Admiral of the Ocean Sea."

"*Sir* Christopher Columbus?" Diego whispered.

The Queen smiled. "Yes, and you shall have the title, too."

"Me? Will I be *Sir* Diego Columbus?"

"Indeed you shall."

Diego and his father bowed low. "Your Majesty," said Christopher, "I thank you most heartily for your faith and for your promise."

The Queen rose. "Go now, Sir Christopher and Sir Diego, to Palos. There is much to be arranged and done before you set sail. May God go with you."

Chapter 4

A Sailor Signs On

*T*he church bell chimed again and again. Diego watched as the people of Palos hurried up the path.

"Has someone died?" a man's voice asked.

"Is it war?" another exclaimed. "Are the Turks coming again?"

"They don't call town meetings every day," a woman said as she picked up a whimpering child. "When they ring the bell, that means it's something important."

"Here comes Pinzón," someone said. "He'll know."

Pinzón stopped at the crest of the hill. The townsfolk gathered around him, pressing him with their questions. Diego edged in close.

"So many worried faces!" Pinzón laughed. "You'd think the Turks had arrived."

"Wouldn't be the first time," a deep voice grumbled.

"True," Pinzón agreed, "but be assured, my friends, we're not at war."

"What's happened then?"

Pinzón scratched his bristly chin. "All I know is that it has something to do with that foreigner, Colbumbus."

Diego felt his cheeks grow hot. He wanted to shout at Pinzón — Pinzón with his arrogant swagger. *You're talking about my father, Sir Christopher Columbus!*

But Diego bit his lip, remembering Friar Juan's advice: *Wait before you speak. An angry burst of words is like the wind that slams a door.*

The church bell rang once more and the door of the church opened. Diego stood on tiptoe, just in front of Pinzón. Three men stepped out of the church. Diego recognized them all. The first was a town official, Francisco Fernández, second in command to the mayor. With him were Friar Juan and Diego's own father.

Fernández called for silence. He unrolled a letter and began to read aloud:

Ferdinand and Isabella, King and Queen by the grace of God, send greetings and grace to the people of Palos.

Know ye that we have commanded Christopher Columbus to go with three ships toward certain regions within the Ocean Sea. And because, in years past, the town of Palos has failed to pay its taxes, the people of Palos are hereby required to provide Sir Christopher with two of those three ships, fully equipped for one year's service. We command that all must be made ready in ten days' time.

Fernández looked up at the crowd. "This edict is signed by Their Royal Majesties, the King and Queen of Spain."

"Two ships?" Pinzón shouted. "In ten days' time? Why not ask for the moon?"

"Silence," Fernández demanded. "There's more. Their Majesties have decreed that all criminal or civil charges will be dropped against anyone who will agree to sail with Admiral Columbus."

"Shall we risk our lives?" an angry voice called out. "Shall we send our sons to sail with murderers and thieves?"

"Who is this man that we should give him ships?"

Fernández banged his wooden staff on the stone steps. "Will you risk an even greater punishment from the Crown? A royal order must be obeyed."

"Columbus needs more than men," someone shouted. "He needs a knife between his ribs."

"*That* would put an end to his dreaming," laughed Pinzón.

Spinning on his heel, Diego grabbed Pinzón's sleeve. "They'll listen to you, Señor. Talk to them. Tell them — "

Pinzón shrugged. "I can't think of any reason *I* should help Col-bumbus."

"Don't then," Diego snapped. "Perhaps you're rich enough already. Or perhaps you're just afraid." He jumped on a bench not far from the door of the church. "Listen, everyone, listen," he shouted. "In the Indies, the rooftops are made of gold. Gold! There are gems to be had for the asking."

A buzz of excitement hummed through the crowd.

"Hold out your empty hands," Diego called out. "Imagine them full of gold. Brave men will sail with Columbus, and the brave will come home rich. Let cowards stay home and count the sardines in their nets!"

"I will go," cried a voice from the back.

Pinzón jumped on the bench beside Diego. "No one shall say that *I* was afraid. Write the name Martín Alonso Pinzón at the top of the list. I shall sail with Columbus. Who else has the courage to go?"

Once again, the churchyard bubbled with talk.

Diego scanned the faces before him. At the edge of the crowd, he saw his father and Friar Juan standing side by side. Friar Juan shook his head, but Christopher Columbus shook all over — with laughter!

Diego grinned. He raised one hand in salute.

The Night Before Sailing

*D*iego and his father stood at the gate of La Rábida, listening to the hoot of owls calling back and forth. In the distance, down the long steep hill, lay Palos and the harbor.

"It's time to say good-bye," Christopher said.

"We should be good at that by now," Diego said bitterly.

"Not again," Christopher groaned. "We've had this discussion a dozen times already. I *can't* let you go. Maybe when you're older — "

"It's not fair," Diego insisted. "I helped you convince the Queen. And look what happened in the church-yard. Even Friar Juan said you'd never have gotten a crew if it hadn't been for me."

"Try to understand," his father sighed. "What you did was wonderful, and I've never denied the power of your tongue. You could convince a frog to fly if you took a mind to . . . but being able to *talk* does not mean that you could survive a long ocean voyage."

Christopher came close, and Diego leaned his head against his father's chest. The two were silent.

"I'll be back," Christopher said softly.

"I know."

"So let's have no more talk about your going."

Diego's face broke into a sudden smile. "All right, Father. No more *talk*."

"Time for me to go," Christopher said softly. "I must be up before dawn to say prayers at the church. We sail with the tide. Will you be there to see me off?"

"I'll be there," Diego promised.

As he watched his father stride down the path, Diego felt the darkness close around him. Turning, he dashed across the courtyard. He pushed open the door of the chapel and went inside. Drawn by the light of burning candles, Diego walked toward the altar. Halfway down the aisle, he stopped and stood in front of a small painted statue.

Friar Juan stepped out from the shadows.

"Tomorrow's the big day," Diego whispered, still studying the marble smile on the saint's face.

"The ships are loaded and ready to go?" asked Friar Juan.

"Yes," Diego answered. He paused. "I wonder if Saint Francis ever did anything wrong."

Friar Juan put his arm around Diego's shoulder. "Francis did *plenty* of things that were wrong. In fact, he was such a wild young man, his father disowned him."

"Maybe I'm like Saint Francis. Only I'm not so much disowned as deserted by my father."

"Come now, Diego," Friar Juan chided. "Deserted, indeed!"

"How *can* he sail without me? On the most important voyage he has ever made? No matter what I say, the answer is no."

"Can't you hear the love in what he says? He's afraid of losing you. Perhaps because of your mother's death, he feels he must protect you."

Diego looked into the priest's round face. "There's a big old tree behind the barn."

"Yes," said Friar Juan. "God made oak trees especially for birds and small boys."

Diego smiled. "Yesterday, I climbed up there to think and I made a decision."

"It sounds important," the priest murmured.

"It is," Diego said. "I decided that I can't just sit on my hands waiting until I'm older and stronger. I have to go on this trip with my father."

"What you *have* to do, young man, is develop

patience," Friar Juan scolded. "You've never had a scrap of it as long as I've known you. Your father has asked me to watch over you until he gets home."

"I *must* go, Friar Juan. Please! Please understand."

Friar Juan tightened his grip around Diego's slender shoulders. "Think carefully, my son."

"I have."

"I believe you have," Friar Juan said sadly. "There have been times in the past few weeks when I could almost see a plan forming inside you — sprouting from your head like horns on a goat."

Diego laughed. "No one knows me better than you."

"Only God, my son," Friar Juan said. He reached into the pocket of his cloak and brought out a silver cross on a chain. Diego bowed his head as Friar Juan slipped it around his neck.

Diego heard a catch in Friar Juan's voice. "This cross belonged to my father. Wear it around your neck wherever you go. And may God be with you."

Friar Juan hurried from the chapel.

Diego knelt down and crossed himself. He prayed for the safety of his father's ships...for the *Pínta*, the *Níña*, and *Santa María*. And then he prayed for himself — and for his plan.

August 3, 1492

*D*iego woke early after a night of fitful dreams. He quickly struck the flint beside his bed and lighted the lamp. He splashed his face with water and dressed, careful not to make any noise as he moved about the room.

Opening the door a crack, he listened and then peeped out. Seeing no one, he slipped from his room and ran down the hall and out the back door. He longed to run all the way from La Rábida down to the harbor.

But the sky was still black, and when Diego came close to the forest, his legs refused to move. His breath came fast. His skin was clammy, wet with sweat. He knew it wasn't just the heat. "Coward," he accused himself. "Baby!"

He remembered the Queen's question: *Are you completely fearless, young man?*

"If you only knew," he whispered. "Your *son*, as you called me, is afraid of the dark! I can no more walk through the forest at night than walk through a field of fire."

Diego trudged back to the chapel steps. Angry and ashamed, he sat down and waited for the dawn.

As the first rays of light streaked the sky, Diego shook off the fears that clawed at him. He hurried across the courtyard and sped through the forest, still shadowed with night.

When at last he reached Palos, Diego slowed his pace. The twisting streets were full of people and carts. By the time he reached the harbor, the square was bristling with life. Dogs barked and chased the sea gulls. Fishermen jostled each other as they lugged their heavy nets down to the water's edge.

Merchants called out their wares. "Sausage! Hot sausage, baked in a bun. If you've got but a penny, then you shall have one."

Diego rummaged in his pocket and found a single coin. "Someday my pocket will jangle, full of coins. Then I shall have all the sausage I want and more! Sausage and biscuits, plums, figs... I shall have them all."

He bought a bun and munched it while he hurried toward the *Santa María*. Scattered along the bank were women who had come to say good-bye. They stood with their children and men too old to sail.

A gray-haired fisherman nudged Diego. "A wonder it is, the ocean itself don't boil in this heat. Day of the halcyon, that's what it is. Mark me, lad, there'll be no wind to fill them sails."

"They can use the oars," Diego protested, "and the tide will pull them downriver, out to sea."

The old man shook his head. "To set sail without the wind is to sail without blessing. Even a fool knows that. And to sail on a Friday, too. Bad luck, it is! Begging for trouble. Even a fool — "

Diego covered his ears. Turning quickly, he waded out knee-deep in the water. He could see, in the gray light of morning, the *Niña* with her three masts leaning back toward the shore. Next to her was the *Pínta*. Diego stood for a moment, watching Pinzón as he marched back and forth along its deck, hands waving as he shouted orders to his men.

Diego splashed on toward the *Santa María*, the biggest of the fleet. Squinting, he recognized his father bounding over the deck — bracing the rigging, testing the lines — as if he were a simple sailor.

And then Diego heard his father's voice. "Hoist the flag!"

The cry was echoed by the men on the other two ships, first the *Pínta* and then the *Niña*. "Hoist the flag! Hoist the flag!"

Diego watched as the admiral's banner hummed to

the masthead, a white banner with a cross in the center. The flag hung limp, like the sails.

At six o'clock sharp, Christopher Columbus called out in a strong, steady voice, "In the name of Jesus, weigh anchor."

"Weigh anchor," the crew called back, and the ships began to move slowly down the river toward the open sea.

Though he knew his father wouldn't see him, Diego waved from the shore.

As the ships slipped out to sea, he could hear the soft plosh-plosh of the oars dipping down again and again. He could hear the fading chant of the men on board. Overhead the sea gulls called.

Diego watched his father's fleet grow smaller and smaller. When the topmost flag dipped out of sight, he splashed up the bank.

"Now it's my turn," he muttered. "Time now that *I* must act."

Chapter 7

Launched

*D*iego walked down the pier. A bearded sailor came toward him, lugging a barrel strapped with iron. Diego stepped into his path.

"Do you need any men?" he asked.

"Aye, but not your size. We've got boys enough to swab the decks. Strong men is what we need." The sailor shoved Diego aside and hurried on.

Diego shrugged. Farther down the wharf, he saw a boy about his age carrying a load of ropes that looped and trailed down his legs like a nest of snakes. Diego fell in step with him.

"Need more hands on your ship?"

"We might," the boy replied. "You can ask the Captain."

Pretending to watch the ships in the harbor, Diego stole glances at the boy who walked beside him. They were about the same age but the other boy was taller. His hands and ears were too big for his body. His long straight hair hung down to his shoulders and almost covered his deep-set eyes.

"My name is José," said the boy.

"I'm Diego. Are you headed out to the islands?"

José nodded. "To the Canaries, then north to Bruges. Want to go along?"

"Only as far as the Canaries," Diego answered. "I have another voyage to take from there."

"Where to?"

Diego dodged the question. "When do you sail?"

"As soon as we've got her loaded," José said. He shielded his eyes against the sun. "Yonder's my ship — the *Dart*. And here comes the Captain. That's him with the blue bandanna around his neck."

"Captain, sir," Diego called out. "Could you use more men aboard ship?"

The Captain was short and thick. Diego thought he looked like one of the barrels that surrounded him on deck. "Speak up," he shouted back, one hand cupped to his ear.

"Ship's boy! Do you need another hand?"

"Could be. Come aboard."

Diego crossed the narrow plank onto the *Dart*. "I'd work hard, sir."

Squinting out of one eye, the Captain looked him over.

Diego bit his lip but kept his eyes on the Captain's face.

"Can you read?"

"Yes — Spanish, Latin, and some French."

"Rich boy, eh! Running away from home, are you?"

"No, sir. I just need to get to the islands."

"All right," the Captain growled. "Be ready to sail in two hours."

"You won't regret it, sir."

"Let's hope not," said the Captain, "but if I do, *you'll* be the one who's sorry."

"Shall I show him the ship?" José asked.

The Captain nodded. "And then get back to work. I have some last-minute business on shore."

"Aye, aye, sir."

Standing on the deck beside José, Diego watched as the Captain strode away. "How many times have you sailed?" he asked.

"Three," José answered. "And all three times aboard the *Dart*."

"The Captain," Diego began, "is he — "

"Don't worry," José broke in. "He's tough, but he's fair. You'll see."

"Have you ever seen him smile?"

"Never."

"It helps when you know what to expect," Diego said with a shrug. "What's in all those barrels?"

"Water. Captain's got 'em lashed down tight. Those over there," José said, pointing, "are full of olive oil, and down below are barrels of wine."

"What will I have to do?"

"Mostly, you'll do what I do. You'll swab the decks,

help the cook, take the Captain his dinner...Oh, and you'll have to learn the chants. The ship's boy must sing a verse at the end of every watch. It's how we mark the time."

Diego thought about the chants he had sung day after day at La Rábida. He could almost hear Friar Juan's high wobbly voice as it blended with Friar Pierre's rich bass. With an effort, he brought his mind back to the ship. "I shall like that part — the singing."

"Good," said José, "come with me. I'll take you below."

Diego had to duck as he followed José down to the lower deck.

"Is there anyone you need to see before we sail?" José asked. "Did you kiss your mother good-bye?"

"The Queen is my mother."

José laughed. "Sure she is, and I was hatched from a sea gull's egg."

Suddenly, the ship lurched. Diego felt it rock, its timbers creaking as the waves pushed it to and fro.

"This is it," he whispered.

"Not yet," said José. "We won't weigh anchor for another hour or more."

"I just meant," Diego stammered, "that . . .well...it has all begun for me."

José frowned. "Listen, if you're going to change your mind, do it now and be done."

Diego shook his head. "Don't worry. I'm ready to sail."

Chapter 8

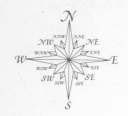

Sickness at Sea

*D*iego held the hourglass in his hand and watched the sand sift down, grain by tiny grain. In the quiet, he could almost hear José's voice, just as he had heard it on that first day aboard: "The most important job of a ship's boy is turning the glass. Every watch is four hours long. The sand will run to the bottom of the glass eight times in the watch. The boy must count the turns and sing the chant when the watch is done. The whole ship, even the Captain, depends on the boy who tells the time."

As the ocean licked at the sides of the ship, Diego's head bobbed in rhythm. His eyelids drooped.

Suddenly, he was jolted awake.

"Move your feet, boy," a sailor snarled as he sloshed the deck with water.

Diego jumped back.

The sailor pulled a wet rag from his wooden bucket. With a smirk, he cracked the cloth like a whip, snapping it again and again at Diego's legs. "Fall asleep on your watch, boy, and you will feel the lash. Thirty strokes on your back! It's a lesson you won't soon forget."

"I wasn't asleep," Diego protested.

"So you say," the sailor laughed as he walked away. "If the Captain knew you were napping — "

"I wasn't!"

Blinking away the sting of tears, Diego looked into the sky. It was almost dawn, and the moon hung just above the horizon, like a thin slice of lemon. As he stared at the moon, Friar Juan's face seemed to take shape there. Diego imagined his old friend at La Rábida. Just about now, Friar Juan would be getting up from his bed. He would cross himself, touching his forehead, chest, and shoulders. Then he would kneel on the hard stone floor of his room.

"Pray for me, Friar Juan," Diego whispered. "I may never see your face again."

Diego held the hourglass up in the half-light. All the sand had sifted down to the bottom of the glass. He took a deep breath and began the chant, singing as loud as he could:

> *Good is that which goes,*
> *Better that which comes.*
> *Seven is past and eight is flowing.*
> *More will flow if God shall will it.*

Chant done, Diego went back to the stern to talk to Sancho, the ship's pilot.

Sancho stood on the poop deck, squinting into the sky. His hands were clasped behind his back, and in his face were furrows plowed by wind and time. Diego thought he looked like a weathered seabird.

"Your watch is done, lad?"

"Almost, and tonight I shall be glad to see it end."

"Long as I've been at sea, I've never stopped the dream of laying my bones on a soft feather bed. Laying me down to sleep — soft. To sleep the whole night through." Sancho kept his eyes on the sky as he spoke. "The wind is good. There should be good sailing today."

"How many days before we reach the Canaries?" Diego asked.

"No one can say for sure. But if this wind holds, we could see land in four good days, maybe five."

"I hope so."

"Got business to see to, have you?" Sancho teased.

Before Diego could answer, he heard footsteps running toward them. It was José.

"Sancho," he called out. "It's the Captain, sir! I went to take him his breakfast, but the Captain... the Captain was sprawled in his chair. Like a man who's been shot! Said he was burning in a hundred fires of hell. Sir, the man's too sick to stand on his feet."

"Steady, lad," Sancho warned. "Was he right in his mind?"

"No, he called me Rodrigo, but he should know me. I've served him three voyages now."

"His cheeks and neck were red?"

José nodded. "And when I gave him some water, his hands shook as he took the cup. Like an old, old man, he was."

"The fever?" Diego whispered.

"The fever," Sancho said grimly. "When it strikes, every child of God lives within the shadow of death. I've known it to strike *every* man and boy aboard ship."

"What can we do?" Diego asked.

Sancho just shook his head. He spoke instead to José. "Go back to the Captain. Take him biscuits soaked in oil. Try to make him eat, a little at a time. Hold a cup to his lips. Let him drink water or whatever he will."

Diego stared at José and saw the fear in his friend's eyes. He knew that it mirrored his own.

Without a word, José turned and disappeared below deck.

Suddenly, the ship lurched, and the mainsail went slack.

Sancho bent over the hatch in the floor of the deck. "Helmsman! To your tiller," he shouted.

Diego peered through the hatch. The helmsman had slumped to his knees, and the tiller turned willy-nilly, first one way and then the other.

"God help us," Sancho gasped. "The helmsman — he's got the fever, too. Diego, go below. Run! Run quickly! Take the tiller. Hold her steady until I come."

Chapter 9

The Fever Takes Its Toll

*D*iego stood on the deck, his legs spread wide. He folded his arms across his chest, hoping no one would notice how his muscles were twitching—how he shivered despite the warm August sun.

"Wind's got a nip in it," José muttered, rubbing his bare arms.

Diego's voice was hoarse. "When do they bring it?"

"The body?"

Diego nodded.

"How should I know?" José snapped. "I've never seen anyone buried at sea before."

"I thought maybe—"

"Well, you thought wrong," José said harshly. His voice then dropped to a whisper. "I've been lucky, I guess. Until now."

Diego bit his lip to keep it from trembling. He closed

his eyes. Beneath his thin shirt he could feel the cool silver of the cross that Friar Juan had given him. "Four days at sea," he murmured, "and one dead already."

Suddenly, an elbow nudged his ribs. José's voice was urgent. "Here they come with Carlos. With the body."

Diego opened his eyes.

Four sailors slowly emerged from the lower deck. Between them they carried a plank, each one grasping a corner edge. On the plank was a large, long canvas sack. The sailors' backs curved over their load.

"Carlos was like a tree trunk," Diego said softly. "Remember that day when Manuel tried to pick a fight with him? Carlos picked him up by his shirt. Held him out over the side of the ship until he begged for mercy."

José smiled. "If Carlos was a tree trunk, then Manuel is a twig."

"A twig that can't swim," Diego added. "He was sure scared that day."

As the four pallbearers trudged past them, the two boys edged back. Diego could see the uneven stitching on the sailcloth sack. Silence followed the body as it was carried across the deck.

Sancho stepped forward. Shuffling and coughing, the circle of men and boys closed in around him.

Sancho cleared his throat. "We are gathered here, in the sight of God in the heavens to say farewell to Carlos, the first of us to die . . ."

Diego's stomach lurched like the topsail in a changing wind. He leaned back against the rail. Who would be next?

Diego glanced at José's face. *He's as pale as sailcloth,* Diego thought.

Sancho's voice was louder now. "We commit our friend Carlos to the deep and to the mercy of heaven."

Sancho traced the shape of a cross over the dead man's body. Then he tipped his head back, squinting into the sun. As he lifted up his hands, the men hoisted their burden to the side of the ship.

Diego hugged himself and looked away. He studied the sky, searching for clouds or sea gulls. But there were no clouds in the hard blue sky, and no gulls so far from shore.

"Heave," said one.

"Heave ho," the others echoed as they lifted the plank on one end.

Diego caught his breath as the canvas slid toward the water.

"Rest in peace," Sancho intoned.

"Rest in peace," murmured the men as they bowed their heads and crossed themselves. Some of them seemed to be saying prayers as they slowly went back to their chores.

Diego stood frozen in place. His throat ached as if he had been shouting for days on end. He felt a hand on his shoulder. Turning, he saw Sancho.

"You were on watch all night, boy," the sailor said kindly. "Get some rest now. We can probably manage the ship for a couple of hours without you."

"I wanted to see if the Captain is . . ."

Sancho nodded. "God willing, he'll live to command this ship once again. Check on him if you like, and then get some sleep."

At the doorway of the Captain's cabin, Diego paused. In the half-light, he could see that someone was there already, standing beside the captain's bunk.

"José?"

"Yes."

"Is he better?"

José shook his head. "See for yourself."

The Captain's breath came in shallow, short puffs. His cheeks and neck were bright red.

"What if he dies?" Diego whispered hoarsely.

José whirled on him, eyes ablaze. "Don't say that!"

"But, look, he's like a scrap of kitchen cloth that caught fire in the flames."

"He *has* to live," José hissed. "If the Captain dies, we all die, and this ship will be our tomb."

"It doesn't have to mean that."

"It *does*! But the Captain won't die. He *won't*."

Diego studied his friend's face and saw the hard line of his jaw pushed out against the fear.

José swiped at his tears. "He's more like a father to me than my real one ever was."

47

"Where *is* your real father?"

José shrugged. "I don't know. What about you? Do you know where *your* father is?"

"My father is a great man."

"I asked you *where*, not who, your father is."

"I don't know," Diego muttered. Turning quickly, he left the Captain's room. On deck, he leaned against the rail and looked down into the churning sea. José's question lapped against his brain again and again. Where *was* Christopher Columbus? What if the *Santa María* had already reached the Canary Islands and then sailed on — with Diego still lost at sea? Would the *Dart* become his tomb as José had predicted?

Chapter 10

Storm at Sea

*D*iego felt hands roughly shaking him. "Wake up, wake up!" said a voice.

"Go away," Diego murmured. "The Queen...she said I could —"

"Diego, wake up! You've got to help."

Diego opened one eye and saw José standing over him, eyes wide with fear.

"There's a storm, a bad one. It came sudden! We've got to shorten sail or we're done for — for sure!"

Diego jumped to his feet and followed José as he ran toward the deck. The *Dart* lurched hard to starboard, tossing the two of them against the curved side of the ship.

Lightning cracked the sky and an angry wind howled her fury. With every gust, the great sails strained, threatening to break the spars and masts that held them.

"Stay low," José shouted. "Hold tight to the rail."

Diego tried to call back to him, but his voice was lost in the storm. He could barely breathe, whipped by battering rain.

On deck, Sancho shouted orders to the men. "Steady does it, men. First the mainsail. Tie her tight." Following Sancho's gaze, Diego saw Mario, Berto, Fermín, and four other sailors high in the rigging. With their feet on ropes hanging from the yard and their chests resting on it, they pulled the sail upward. They looked like huge insects as they gathered the sail and lashed it to the yard. Squinting, Diego watched them gather up length after length of rain-soaked canvas, binding it tightly with rope.

Suddenly, the *Dart* was lifted to the top of a huge foaming wave. Diego felt it stop, teetering on the crest, before it tipped and crashed down into the trough. The *Dart* wallowed, almost flat on her side for a moment. Waves crashed onto the deck. All the men were shouting. Some cursed and some prayed.

Diego lost hold of the rail. He felt himself slipping, sliding toward the raging waves. The ship itself seemed to spin. He thrust out both arms, grabbing at anything that might stop him from being washed into the sea.

At last Diego's fingers caught a coil of rope that was lashed to the mast. He twisted his body onto it, clutching it with both hands and wrapping his legs in the coils of rope.

Holding tight, Diego looked up. Above him, Berto, Mario, Fermín, and the others hung suspended in the rigging, high above the churning waves.

"God help us, God save us," Diego whispered over and over.

Gradually, the wind slackened its fury, and the *Dart* began to right itself in the water. As *up* became *up* once again, the sailors set to work tying the final knots to secure the sail.

Diego watched the four men on the first team inch their way down the skeleton mast. He thought about his father: *What would he be doing if he were aboard the Dart?*

He knew the answer. Christopher Columbus would never stand and watch. *He* would be scrambling up the rigging, sucking in danger like most men breathe air.

"Good work, men," Sancho shouted. "Now the foresail."

Hunching his shoulders against the rain, Diego ran to the forward mast and began to climb the web of rope that stretched to the top of the mast. Beside him, on either side, were Manuel and Berto.

"Get down! Get back, boy," Sancho commanded. "You're too small to fight that wind."

Diego pretended not to hear. His feet fumbled to find the ladder holes. His hands slipped as he grasped the wet ropes, but he kept climbing.

Just as Diego reached the spar, the wind began to howl like a hundred horns, circling the sky and calling out for war.

Beside and below him, voices shouted, "Hold! Hold on!" His hands and arms ached, and his brain felt swollen with fear. The mast creaked and groaned.

Suddenly, the sky flashed bright with light, and a clap of thunder shook the ship. Diego heard a crack — the jagged sound of splintered wood. The mast gave way beneath him, and Diego felt himself falling, falling toward the churning sea.

Chapter II

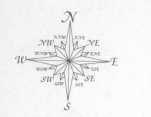

Rescue

*D*iego dropped like an apple falling from a tree. He caught a gasp of air before water closed over his head, rushing into his ears and nose.

Churning! Murky! Dark!

Diego felt his body being dragged and held down by the power of the waves. But then a fire ignited inside him — the fire to live. He pumped his arms and, thrusting his legs apart, he kicked hard again and again.

Diego opened his eyes to slits. A pattern of lights shimmered above him. He blew out the pent-up breath in his lungs and rose through the bubbles toward the light.

Almost ... can make it ... now, now! A powerful kick shot him upward.

Whoomphh!

Diego's body thumped to a stop, crumpled with pain. Desperate for air, he reached up and clutched the sodden rope that coiled above his head.

A heavy web of rigging pressed him down like drowning hands. It tangled in his fingers. Panic swirled inside him. He grasped a coil of rope with both hands and pushed. The web only grew thicker, shoving him deeper.

Diego's chest throbbed. Soon he must breathe in water and then he would die. But once again, the fire licked through his limbs. He fought free of the ropes, then swam until light fanned out above him.

Diego's chin lifted as his face broke the surface. Air! His body was taut. Gasping, he filled his aching lungs.

"Thank God," he murmured over and over. He knew he had been saved, at least for a moment. But when he looked around, he saw that, although he had escaped the rigging, he was far away from the *Dart*. He scanned the crippled ship. The broken mast pointed like a huge bent finger into the sea. Hanging from it was the foresail. Soaked and torn, it seemed to be sinking deeper and deeper into the water.

Over the roar of wind and sea, Diego heard a voice calling out for help. Fighting to keep his head above the waves, he twisted in the water.

He heard the voice again, weaker this time, calling, "For God's sake, help! Help me!"

It seemed to come from beneath the rigging. Swimming toward the sound, Diego saw a face bobbing in and out of sight. It was Manuel, trapped beneath the rigging, his hands clutching the ropes above his head.

"Manuel, let go," Diego shouted. "Swim down."

"Help me!"

"Let go, Manuel. Let go the ropes."

Suddenly the sailor's face dropped from sight. Only the top of his head and the fingers of one hand, still entwined in the tangled line, were visible.

Then Diego remembered. *Manuel can't swim.*

"I'm coming," he shouted. He sucked in a great breath of air and, dodging splintered bits of the mast, dived down.

He could see Manuel's body hanging limp from the rigging with one hand still clinging to the web of rope above him.

Just then, Manuel released his grip. Before Diego's eyes, he dropped until only the ripples showed where he had been.

Diego swam after him, at war with death and the churning sea. Over and over, Diego dived, came up for a breath of air, and then tried again. Finally, exhausted, he knew that the battle was over.

Manuel was dead, but *he* was still alive. He must get back to the ship!

Diego spotted a scrap of wood and swam toward it. It was a barrel lid. He clutched it and heaved his body across it.

Choking, sobbing, he shouted into the wind, "No, no, no!"

Diego rested his cheek on the rough boards. He longed to sleep, but to sleep would be to die. He must get back to the ship or else he'd be lost. He would drown, like Manuel.

In the distance, he spotted the *Dart* bouncing like a wooden toy on the horizon. There was nothing else to see — no other ships, no harbor, no hope — except the *Dart*.

With the barrel lid tucked under his chest, Diego kicked toward the crippled ship. His legs ached and his breath burned in his chest, but still he pressed on.

Slowly, slowly, the *Dart* grew larger. It listed to one side, dragged downward by the weight of the broken mast and its heavy burden of sodden sail. Gradually, Diego was able to make out the shapes of the men on board.

Sancho and Fermín were desperately chopping at the broken mast, trying to free the ship from its deadly weight. He heard a loud crack and saw the mast fall away. The men cheered as the ship began to right itself in the water.

And then he heard someone calling his name. "Diego!" José shouted. "Sancho, come quick. It's Diego. He's alive!"

Other voices chimed in. "Hold on, lad."

"God love you, boy, you're almost safe."

"Hold on! Hold on!"

"Catch the line, boy. You can do it!"

Diego's head began to spin. Dizziness enfolded him, closing over his senses.

Through the fog in his brain, he heard José calling, "Don't give up, Diego."

And Sancho, "The line, Diego, the line! Grab the line."

Diego forced open his eyes. Beside him was the end of rope that Sancho had tossed across the waves. Diego lunged for it and clutched it in both hands.

Diego's body sped through the water. Like a fish that is caught and pulled in, he felt himself being hauled over the side.

He closed his eyes. There were hands. Voices. And a blanket tucked around him.

Splotches of red and purple swirled, spinning in his brain. Then blackness covered it all, and Diego's world disappeared.

Chapter 12

Lost

"Stir that pot, lad," said Salvador, the ship's steward.

Diego grasped the smooth wooden paddle with both hands and stirred. His cheeks and arms stung from the heat of the open firebox, and his eyes smarted. The smells of salt beef, garlic, and hot oil mingled, filling the air with pungent smoke. Diego's stomach rumbled.

"Have you become a bear now," Salvador teased, "growling for your food?"

"It's been a long time since yesterday's lentils."

"Your duel with Master Death has made you hungry."

"Please, Salvador," Diego exclaimed, "the meat is hot and the watch will soon end."

"You don't like to hear talk of death, do you?"

Diego shook his head. "It's over, and I'm alive."

"For now," Salvador said grimly. "But the fever's not done with the *Dart*."

"How can you say that? You don't *know*. Perhaps no more will die."

"Perhaps," Salvador conceded.

Diego speared a chunk of bread that was warming beside the fire. "I'm not ready to be food for fish."

"Death may not *ask* if you're ready," Salvador chuckled. "The stew is done, boy."

Diego lifted the bubbling pot from the fire and slowly carried it into the galley, struggling to keep it from tipping.

The sailors were waiting. "Hurry up," one shouted, banging his bowl on the table.

"That kettle is bigger than he is."

Diego set it down with a thump.

Berto leaned across the table. "Looks like you chopped up your belt and cooked it."

"Nobody's making you eat it," Salvador growled as he placed a pot of rice next to the meat. "Sing, Diego."

"Sing, boy," chorused the men. "We're all starvin' half to death."

Diego began the chant that he'd been taught:

Table, table, sir captain and master — good company, all. Long live the King of Castile by land and by sea! Who says to him *war*, off with his head. Who won't say *amen*, gets nothing to drink. The table is ready. And who don't come, won't eat.

As Diego called out the last words, the men pulled their knives from their sheaths and closed in on the food, each one stabbing a chunk of stringy, gray-brown meat for his bowl.

Diego filled his bowl with steaming rice and beef. He sat next to Berto on the floor and leaned against a barrel.

"Ten days now, you've been at sea," said Berto.

Diego tore at his food, using his fingers and teeth. "Just another day or so to the Canaries."

Berto wiped his mouth on his sleeve. "Another day or so? Sure! Here we are in a crippled ship. Ever since that storm, nobody knows for sure where we are or where we're headed. Captain's sick and nine men down with the fever. There's five of us dead already."

"Eighteen men are alive and well," Diego cried. "We'll make it!"

"If the fever don't take us all."

"It won't," Diego said fiercely. "Nothing else can happen. We've *had* our share of bad luck."

Sancho, sitting across the galley, got to his feet. "Hush, boy," he commanded. "Never tempt fate with words like that."

Chapter *13*

A Shift in the Sails

*D*iego and José sat cross-legged, facing each other. On the deck between them lay the torn canvas they were mending.

Diego held his needle up to the light and carefully threaded it. "My mother used to make shirts for my father and me. She could even make lace."

"But she died?"

"When I was five," said Diego softly. "I'll never forget that night. My father was away, and when they told me she was dead, I wouldn't believe them. I shouted at them... told them she wasn't dead. And then I started to run. The next thing I knew, I was lost — all alone in the forest, and it was dark."

"How long before they found you?" José asked.

"I don't know. It could've been an hour. It felt like a week. What I remember is the dark... the dark." Diego looked down and pushed the needle through the thick cloth.

"And now you claim the Queen for your mother."

"That's right. Because she has claimed me."

José looked up from his work. "Did you really see the Queen? Face-to-face?"

"See her? José, I touched her! Queen Isabella held my hands. She has the softest skin in all the world and red hair like my father's."

"You expect me to believe all that?"

Diego smiled. "It's true. There are things I haven't told you about my father."

"You talk about this voyage you have to take, but you never tell where or why...We're lost, Diego! What good are your secrets *now*?"

"I didn't want anyone to know my plan, not even you or Sancho."

"Because of your father?"

Diego got to his feet, staring out to sea. "Yes, but you're right. I might as well tell you. My father's name is Christopher Columbus. Sir Christopher! He's on his way to the Indies, commissioned by the Queen. He will be the first to go there by sailing west." Diego faced his friend. "Imagine! After his voyage, the world will change. There'll be no more ships sailing the long way around Africa, and all because of my father."

"Didn't you want to go?"

"Want to? Yes! I begged to go, but he said no."

"Why?"

Diego shrugged. "He says I'm not strong, except when I'm talking."

"He should have seen you in that storm."

"Yes, he should have," Diego agreed. "Anyway, I had a plan. I'd sail to the Canaries on the *Dart*. Once there, I'd keep out of sight while my father restocked the ships, and then on the night before sailing, I'd sneak aboard."

"Stow away on your own father's ship?"

"Why not? After a day or two, it wouldn't matter even if I got caught. My father would never sail *back* to the islands — no matter how angry he might be."

"You didn't figure on the fever or the storm."

"No, and by now, my father's ships may have left the Canaries. And here we are, drifting."

"Remember what Salvador said?" José murmured.

Diego nodded. "We're somewhere south of heaven, somewhere north of hell."

"What are you going to do?"

"Do? What *can* I do," Diego sighed, "except wait and pray?"

Just then a familiar face appeared from below deck.

"José, look," Diego exclaimed, "It's the Captain!"

The two boys bounded across the pile of canvas and ran to meet the Captain as he shuffled toward them. Each of them took an arm.

"God be praised, Captain," José exclaimed. "You're walking!"

"Just barely."

"Take it slow, sir," said Diego. "José and I won't let you fall."

"The fever left me, sudden," the Captain mused. "Like stepping out of the fires of hell and into a soft sea breeze. I don't even know how long — "

"You fell sick on the sixth of August," said Diego. "Today is the nineteenth."

"Have we lost any men?"

"Five are dead, and nine more sick, sir," José reported.

"There was a storm," Diego added. "The forward mast is broken."

"Help me to the quarterdeck," the Captain commanded.

Diego and José obeyed, inching along to match the Captain's pace. His breath came in labored gasps.

Standing at the bow, hands clasped behind his back, the Captain sniffed the air like a hunting dog, and his eyes scanned the sky.

Diego and José waited silently.

"Yes," the Captain murmured. "I can feel it in my bones. We're right."

"We're not lost then?" Diego whispered.

"Lost?" the Captain scoffed. "The *Dart*? Don't be foolish, boy."

Suddenly, from the top of the mast, Berto called out, "Land ho! To port. Land! Land in sight to port."

The Captain studied the compass set in the binnacle. "Swing 'er south," he commanded, "one quarter of the southwest wind."

"Swing 'er south, one quarter of the southwest wind," José shouted.

"*Says* the Captain," Diego called out.

Sancho came running, his face wreathed with smiles. "The Captain? Aye, sir. Right you are, sir!"

A cheer went up from the men on deck as they strained against the lines. The ship groaned and creaked as the mainsail filled, puffing out like a peacock's breast.

Diego scrambled up the rigging to the top of the mast. Squinting into the light of the setting sun, Diego saw it — a bead of land in the distance.

"I see it, sir!"

The Captain smiled. "Yes, and what does it look like, boy?"

Diego shouted with joy. "Like hope, sir! It looks like hope!"

Chapter 14

Diego Goes Ashore

A rope ladder hung down the side of the *Dart*. Diego stood on the deck waiting.

"Are you sure you won't change your mind?" José asked.

"I *have* to go," Diego declared.

"But you said yourself — you've seen no sign of your father's ships."

"The *Dart* is sailing on to Gomera, but Father planned to come *here*. I heard him tell Friar Juan he'd restock the fleet in the islands, stopping first at Las Palmas. So that's where I need to be."

The Captain stood beside José. "Save your breath, José. His mind is made up." Leaning on the rail, he spoke to Diego. "Remember this, boy. In Las Palmas, you'll be one more harbor rat — no more. No one will know your name, nor care. No one will give a rotten fig whether you live or die."

Diego shivered. "I'll be careful."

"See to it. And remember what I told you — we're off now to the island of Gomera to replace the mast. Forests of huge sturdy trees are there, I'm told. As soon as we have a new mast, we'll come back here. Watch the harbor, lad. One of these days you'll see the *Dart*. And if you're ready when we come, you can sail north with us to Bruges."

Diego shook the Captain's hand. "Thank you, sir. Thank God you're well again!" He turned to José. "Take good care of him."

Sancho waited down below in the rowboat bouncing in the waves. "Don't take all day, lad. I've got to get back — "

Diego made his way down the ladder and settled himself in the boat, facing Sancho.

Sancho grasped the oars in both hands. "Do you have your wages?"

"Here," said Diego as he patted the bulge beneath his shirt. "They could have to last me a very long time."

"Aye. Guard them well."

The little boat swished through the water, and soon the faces of José and the Captain grew small.

José waved.

Diego waved back, lifting both arms in a last farewell.

"What now for you, lad?" Sancho asked softly. "What will you do?"

Diego cleared his throat. "First, I guess I'll ask around . . . find out if my father has already been to Las

Palmas. And if he's come and gone, I have no choice. I'll wait for the *Dart* to come back."

"*If* your father has come and gone?" Sancho exclaimed. "If? Use your head! It's been nearly three weeks since we left Palos."

"We sailed on the same day as my father."

"Why should your father still be docked in Las Palmas? The *Dart* was lost for nearly two weeks."

"Perhaps his ships had troubles, too."

"And your father just *happened* to end up here at the very same time? In the very same place? Of all the Canary Islands, he ended up here? Come now, lad!"

Diego's voice dropped low. "Something in me says my father won't leave without me. I'm destined for this voyage."

"Destined, indeed," Sancho scoffed. "But what can I say when you talk like that? Only the morrow can say who's right and who's wrong. Only the morrow can say."

Tears, unbidden, filled Diego's eyes. He swiped at them with his wrist, staring out at the passing waves.

Soon the little boat hit the shore. As it wedged itself into the sand, Diego and Sancho jumped out.

"Fare thee well then, son," said the old man. He clasped Diego in a sudden, hasty hug, then climbed back into the boat.

"Thank you," Diego muttered, "for everything."

Quickly, he gave the rowboat a shove. Sancho nodded and began to paddle back to the *Dart*.

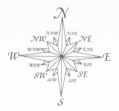

Chapter 15

Nighttime in Las Palmas

*E*ven standing in the street outside, Diego could feel the waves of heat that pulsed from the ironmonger's shop in Las Palmas. He leaned through the doorway.

Rows of iron tools hung from the walls, and a blacksmith stood beside his fire. Sweat glistened on his reddened cheeks. His hammer pounded in rhythm.

"Need some help?" the blacksmith called between blows.

"I'm looking for someone," Diego shouted. "Christopher Columbus, sailing aboard the *Santa María*. Have you seen or heard of him?"

"Columbus, you say? Can't say that I have, but most seamen *do* come in here, sooner or later." The fire blazed higher in the grate, and the blacksmith bent over his work.

Diego left the shop.

Outside a young man leaned against the wall. He was tall and thin, and his mouth pulled down on one side. Nineteen, maybe twenty years old, Diego guessed. His eyes were half-closed, and his arms were folded across his chest.

"Looking for work?" he asked.

"I'm looking for... for a friend," Diego stammered.

The young man shrugged. "Perhaps you've found one."

"It was someone special. A certain person —"

"Oh, I thought maybe you needed work."

"Not right now."

"You have some money then?" said the young man with a grin. "So where have you looked — to find this friend?"

"I've been asking around the shops since morning."

"And no one's seen him?"

"No one. Not yet, anyway."

"That's too bad," the young man said as he pushed away from the wall. "I wish you good luck. You'll need it."

As evening draped Las Palmas in shadows, Diego began to look for a place to sleep. He had to find somewhere safe, out of sight. He spotted a shed in the alley beside a shoemaker's shop, and he ducked inside. It was deserted and smelled of leather.

Feeling his way in the half-light, Diego found a stack of leather strips. Brushing away the cobwebs that clung to his face and neck, he sat down. He reached into his pocket and pulled out two chunks of cheese and a piece of bread. He ate it all, licking the crumbs from his fingers.

Still hungry, Diego patted the pouch that held his wages. "Tomorrow," he promised himself, "I shall have a great big sausage for breakfast."

He yawned. His eyelids drooped, but sleep would not come. From the rafters, he heard the skitter of tiny feet. Rats! He remembered what the Captain had said: *In Las Palmas, you'll be one more harbor rat, and no one will give a rotten fig whether you live or die.*

As it grew darker inside the shed, Diego began to tremble. His breath came fast. "Don't be a baby," he muttered. "What would Father say? *He's* not afraid of the dark."

Diego took a deep breath and began his prayers. When he finished, he opened his eyes. The black of night was closing in like a thick blanket over his head. His heart drummed inside his chest. "Can't," he gasped. "I can't!"

He jumped to his feet and stumbled out the door and into the alley.

Flushed with fear and shame, Diego made his way through the streets. He found a narrow doorway and hunched down, glad for the moon that made a pool of light on the cobblestones beside him.

He listened. Only the pigeons seemed to be awake now. There had been pigeons in Palos. Pigeons, sea gulls, Friar Juan, Pinzón... *Where was Pinzón?* he wondered. At last Diego fell asleep.

His dreams were suddenly shattered as rough hands rolled him over, thumping him out of the doorway into the street.

"That's him," someone said calmly. Diego heard footsteps as the man quickly walked away.

Two other men had emerged from the shadows. The first, much bigger than the other, grabbed Diego's wrists and held them both in one huge hand. With the hand that was free, he covered Diego's mouth.

Desperate, Diego tried to bite and twist away.

"Julio," the smaller man barked. "Hold him."

Julio jabbed his knee into Diego's shoulder, pressing him into the cobblestones.

The second robber grabbed the pouch that held Diego's earnings. "Aha," he snorted, "the very thing we need!"

Diego fought with his legs, kicking as hard as he could. And then he saw the knife glimmering in the moonlight. He froze.

"Smart boy," snarled the robber. "Finally figured it out, eh?" He held the blade up to the light. "You don't

really want me to show you how sharp this is — or do you?"

"Uhhh-unhh," Diego grunted, eyes wide with fear. He heard a snap as the knife cut the cord at his waist.

"Thank you, young sir," said the robber. He jangled the pouch of coins in Diego's face.

"Come on," said Julio. "Let's go."

The two men ran down the street, disappearing in the shadows.

As the sound of their footsteps faded away, Diego inched back into the doorway. Trembling, he tucked his knees to his chest and felt the cool, hard silver of the cross that hung from his neck.

"I'm alive," he whispered. "Thank God, I'm still alive!"

Chapter 16

August 22, 1492

*T*he sun shone down on Diego's face, warming him awake. His whole body ached. His wrists were bruised and sore. He slowly got to his feet, wondering that he had slept at all. Peering out from the doorway, he checked the street in both directions.

He saw a young girl coming toward him, pushing a cart.

"Bread," she chanted, "fresh bread, baked this very morning. Bread, fresh bread, baked this very day."

A woman, her hair wrapped in a blue bandanna, stepped into the street and called, "Elena, here, come back."

Laughing, the girl ran to her with a loaf of bread in each hand. "Never you fear, Senora. I always save two loaves for you."

Diego's stomach rumbled. Instinctively, he felt for the spot where his money pouch had hung. Gone! All that remained was a stinging cut where the robber's knife had nicked his skin.

He stood in the street and watched the girl walk away. He sniffed, savoring the smell that lingered in the air. If only he had one slice!

Behind him, Diego heard a snicker. "Hungry?"

He whirled around. There stood the tall young man from the day before. Again, his arms were folded across his chest, his eyes half-closed. But this time a smile of victory stretched his lips.

"What are *you* laughing at?" Diego demanded.

Opening his hands, the young man blinked rapidly. "I was just amused to see you again. Quite a coincidence! Big town like this. Where are you headed?"

"The harbor."

"Still looking for that friend of yours?"

Diego nodded. "He could be here by now."

The man bent down, eye-to-eye with Diego. "I'll bet you're hungry," he said. "I'll tell you what . . . you come with me. I'll give you a little something to eat, then maybe I'll help you find your friend."

"You'll help me?"

"Sure. By the way, Hawk is my name."

"Hawk?"

The man's face twisted. He clawed the air with his fingers. "You know — Hawk! That bird that swoops down and tears the flesh of little mice."

Diego shivered and pulled away.

Hawk stood straight. "Don't be scared," he said lightly. "I was just teasing. Look at you, you're shivering!"

Diego rubbed the goose bumps on his arms.

"Come along. You'll feel better after you've eaten. My mother is home right now frying up a big batch of fish."

"She won't mind if you bring me along?"

"Mother loves little boys," Hawk laughed. "You'll see."

Diego had to run to keep pace with Hawk's long legs, following him through the narrow streets to a part of town where small houses crowded close together.

Hawk stopped beside an archway almost hidden with vines. Behind it, Diego could see a stone staircase twisting into blackness at the top.

Hawk jerked his head to the right. "Go on," he commanded.

Diego paused. And then he felt an iron grip on his arm — squeezing, bruising the flesh.

"Go on, I said."

The steps were narrow, and the doorway at the top was low. Diego ducked down to enter.

The room was round, like a tower, and dark —
lighted only by a small oil lamp and the glow from one
small, high window. Littered with the remains of food,
it smelled of rotting fruit.

"Hawk," someone called out. "You brought us back a
souvenir."

Squinting into the half-light, Diego saw two men in
the room. Their faces swam in his memory — the two
who had attacked him and taken all his money! One
was big with an ugly bruise on his chin; the other was
so thin that his bones stuck out in his shoulders and
arms.

Diego's cheeks flushed hot. Head spinning, he
searched the room. He had to get out! He crouched,
ready to run.

Behind him, a door slammed shut, and Diego heard
the scrape of an iron key turning in its lock.

Hawk strutted toward him, dangling the key in front
of Diego's face.

"You're with them!" Diego accused.

"Not really. They're with *me*. You might as well sit
down. You aren't going anywhere. You're one of the
gang now, like it or not."

"He's a baby, Hawk," one of the robbers complained.
"Couldn't you find someone big and strong?"

Hawk did not smile. "I know what I'm doing,
Weasel."

"Course you do," Weasel said quickly. His right eye twitched. "I didn't mean nothing."

"An innocent face could be quite useful. Someone to charm our victims and get himself invited home."

"Always thinking, ain't you, Hawk?"

"Ummmh! That's why I'm the boss instead of you."

"Yeah," said the third robber, scratching his broad chest. "You're the boss all right."

"Julio," Hawk snapped, "get him something to eat. Seems he lost his money somehow."

Weasel's laugh was shrill. "Careless of him! Lost his money, eh?"

Diego stared, remembering the greedy look on Weasel's thin face as he had snipped the cord around Diego's waist and touched the small money pouch to his lips.

Julio shuffled across the room, a small chunk of cheese in his big dirty hand.

"That's it now," said Hawk. "That's your food for the day."

"One piece of cheese?" Diego exclaimed. "I'll starve!"

"You won't starve in one day," Hawk said calmly. "Besides, Julio will be here. *He'll* take care of you."

"Like a mother," Julio mocked.

"Before too long, he'll be ready to work — and eat," Weasel predicted.

"Never!" Diego muttered.

Hawk stood in the doorway, key in hand. "You can start by cleaning the floor," he snarled. "Me and Weasel, we've got business to do."

"I'll see to him, boss," Julio promised.

As the key turned in the lock, Julio shoved a bucket toward Diego. "Here's water and a rag. Get busy."

Diego said nothing. He knelt down and began to scrub. By the time he had finished, Julio was snoring. Exhausted and sore from his bruises, Diego found an old blanket, curled up on the floor, and fell asleep.

The Window

*D*iego lay on the floor of the tower room. In the moonlight that shone through the one small window, he could see the remains of supper left on the table and fish bones that had dropped to the floor. Hawk had only laughed when Diego asked for food — just a small piece of fish, a chunk of bread. Now there was nothing left, only the smells of fish and sweat.

Wide awake from hunger and fear, Diego listened to the robbers as they snored and shifted in their beds. Questions spun in his brain. *Would he ever get away? And where was his father tonight?* No answers came, only more questions.

Toward morning, Diego got up. He crept past the sleeping thieves and picked up a small bench. Slowly and carefully, he carried it across the room and set it beneath the open window. He paused, listening to the buzz of sleep, then climbed up and looked out.

From his perch, Diego could see the harbor in the distance — white sails against a pale dawn sky. The streets below were deserted, except for two fishermen and a small ragged dog.

Suddenly, Diego's heart began to pound. Coming up the hill was a priest. His head was shaved above his ears, and he wore a gray robe, just like the one that Friar Juan wore. Around his neck was a large silver cross.

The priest and the fishermen stopped to talk. When they parted ways, the priest walked beneath the window and up the hill.

Diego longed to call out to him but dared not wake Hawk and the others. Standing on tiptoe, Diego searched the skyline above the tangle of houses and streets. Although the priest had disappeared, he saw what he was looking for — a church spire reaching toward heaven, like hands pressed together in prayer.

Diego whispered a prayer. "O Lord, look down on your child. Have mercy, have mercy."

"What d'you think you're doing?" a voice demanded.

Weasel was awake.

Diego gripped the window ledge. "Nothing," he said softly. "I couldn't sleep."

"Too bad you're a mouse and not a bird. If you were a bird, you'd flap your wings and be gone."

"I'd be gone all right," Diego said bitterly.

Weasel laughed and rolled over.

Diego waited a while to be sure Weasel was asleep again. Then he leaned out the window as far as he could without jumping up or making noise. If a bird could fly away, he reasoned, surely a mouse could find some way to escape.

Below the window, he saw the steep slope of the roof. At its base, it touched a wall embedded with jagged iron spikes.

No one, Diego thought, *could climb over that wall, but someone small might find a way to get through those spikes. Down and off and free!*

He smiled. "Come the dawn, I'll find a way somehow."

Julio laid a huge hand on Diego's shoulder. "I say we take him with us."

"And I say we don't," Weasel snapped. "Like as not, he'd make a run for it."

Hawk held up both hands, crooking his fingers like claws. "But if our little mouse runs, he knows Hawk will catch him." He snarled and ripped the air with his claws. "No matter where he hides, Hawk will find his mouse."

"And then there's no more mouse," said Weasel gaily.

"Lock him in," Hawk decided. "Before long, he'll be ready to cooperate, and then we'll let him eat like one of the gang."

Diego said nothing. He sat in the corner of the room, waiting for the men to leave. When at last the door closed behind them, he ran to the window. Standing on the bench, he saw the tops of their heads — Julio, Weasel, and Hawk — as they made their way down the street.

As soon as the robbers were out of sight, Diego looked out toward the sea. The very sight of ships, clustered in the harbor, made him feel better. And then he saw it — a ship with a dark red cross on a pure white sail. Above the arms of the cross were the initials of the King and Queen of Spain. That cross was on every sail in his father's fleet of three!

Breathless, Diego squinted into the sunlight. It was the *Pínta*.

The Pínta! That means Pinzón is here!

Quickly, Diego studied the roof below the window's edge. It looked farther away than it had in the half-light of dawn and angled down sharply toward the murderous spikes.

Diego pulled off his shirt and tore it in strips. Binding the pieces together, he formed a short rope and tied it around his waist.

He hoisted himself onto the window ledge. Shifting his weight to one side, he slung one knee up. Inching over the ledge, he straddled it. Then swinging his weight over, he balanced on the window ledge — feet out, head in.

"If only . . . I could fly," he panted.

Too late to become a bird. Too late to be afraid.

Diego eased himself down, down until the ledge cut into his chest. He pushed off and hung suspended from the window frame, his hands slipping.

"Now," he whispered and let go. Bending his knees against the fall, Diego thumped to the red clay roof below.

For a moment he lay breathless. And then he arched his back like a cat, hunched on his hands and knees, and began to back toward the wall, inch by inch. Below him were the spikes.

Chapter 18

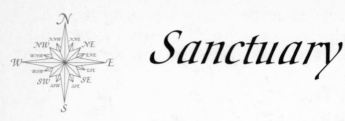

Sanctuary

*H*alfway down the sloping roof, Diego's foot slipped, skidding against a curving edge of tile. A roof tile broke and tumbled to the street, echoing on the cobblestones below.

"What was that?" a woman's voice exclaimed.

Diego held his breath and flattened himself against the tiles.

A man answered, "A cat. Just a cat."

"Someone's up there," the woman warned.

The man began to laugh. "You're always imagining things: thieves in the pantry, burglars on the roof..."

"It *wasn't* a cat," the woman insisted as the two walked away.

Diego listened until their voices and footsteps faded. He eased himself down to the lower edge of the roof. No one must see him. No one. Crouching, he took the handmade rope from his waist and tied it to the base of the nearest spike.

Suddenly, Diego heard Weasel's high-pitched laugh in the street below him. He peered over the ledge and saw them: Julio, Weasel, and Hawk. Soon they would unlock the door upstairs. They'd see the open window and a "mouse" trembling on the roof — easy prey for a Hawk!

Diego held his breath as the three men passed beneath him and went inside. He knew his life was measured, not in minutes but in seconds lost or won. He grasped the rope and pushed off, letting it slide through his hands. He dangled at its end, then dropped.

As he landed, his ankle twisted between the cobblestones.

From inside the house came a roar from Julio. "He's gone. The boy's gone!"

Shaking off pain, Diego began to run, clutching the cross that hung on his chest.

He heard Hawk shout. "Don't just stand there. Find him! *Get* him!"

Diego ducked into a side street. Just ahead were a horse and a wagon filled with hay. He leaped into it, burrowing down.

He heard Weasel's voice. They were in the street now. "Where could he be?"

Diego dared not move, despite the tickles of the itching hay.

"Idiots!" snapped Hawk. "Don't everyone follow *me*. Spread out. Julio, you check up here. Weasel and me, we'll go down to the harbor. That's where the boy said he was going in the first place."

The wagon began to move.

Diego peeped through the slats. He saw Julio standing in the middle of the street, scratching his head. The wagon turned a corner and slowly rattled uphill.

Turning once again, the wagon thumped onto a dirt road. Diego lay still until it stopped. He rose, brushing hay from his shoulders and head.

A farmer, pitchfork in hand, ran toward him shouting, "Come here, you!"

Diego jumped down from the wagon. Wherever the road led *up*, he ran. The priest had made his way uphill... At last, Diego dared to slow his pace. He looked, and in the distance, he saw the fingers of the church, pointing up to God.

Again and again, Diego clanged the bell at the church door. The door creaked open and a puzzled face appeared.

"It wasn't locked, son. You might've come on in."

"Not locked?" Diego gasped. "I was — "

"Frightened. Of course you were, but you're safe now."

Diego slipped into the cool dark of the church. "Father, I need — "

"Sanctuary. A place to hide, somewhere you can be safe for a time. *And* you need a shirt. Follow me."

Diego drank in the smells of incense, candle wax...and best of all, the scent of safety.

"I'm Friar Guillermo," said the priest as he padded down the long aisle of the nave. "And you are — "

"Hungry, Father. Very hungry."

Friar Guillermo laughed. "I was asking your name, but come along. Cook is making a stew for our lunch. I'm sure there's plenty for you as well."

All of a sudden, Diego could walk no farther. Rivers of fear and relief converged and rose up inside him. Overflowing their banks, spilling...

He dropped to his knees and sobbed.

Friar Guillermo knelt beside him, one gentle hand resting on Diego's back. "It's all right. Let the tears fall. Our Lord himself wept sometimes... You're safe now, son. You're safe."

Diego sighed deeply. "There's something, something — "

"Take your time," Friar Guillermo crooned, plucking bits of hay from Diego's hair. "The time for running is over. All over and done."

"Not yet. There's something I must do, and quickly. I need your help."

"Yes?"

Diego fought to control his voice. "I must get a message to someone...Martín Alonso Pinzón. He's the captain of the *Pínta,* just now sailing into port."

Father Guillermo frowned. "Surely, you mustn't go — "

"No, *that* would not be safe."

"Very well. I'll go myself, right after lunch." The priest patted his round belly and struggled to his feet.

"Thank you, sir!"

"Your thanks belong to God, son," Friar Guillermo chided gently. "Now what is the message for Captain Pinzón?"

"Tell him...tell him this: Come to the church at dawn. Columbus will be waiting."

Chapter 19

Meeting at Dawn

*D*uring the night, a heavy fog had settled on Las Palmas, draping the town in white netting, hiding the ships in the harbor.

Diego stood in the doorway of the church, listening for human sounds.

Silence.

He slipped out and closed the door behind him. Darting across the pathway, he ran into the graveyard beside the church and ducked down behind a gray tombstone. From there, he had a good view of the road from town. Pinzón would have to come that way. So, too, would Hawk if he should come looking for his mouse.

In his mind's eye, Diego could see Hawk's snarling lip and the long, thin fingers crooked like claws.

Think of something else, Diego told himself, *something good. Imagine three ships heading out to sea. White sails, each one with a dark red cross...Three ships pushed by a strong, good breeze, and a boy aboard, standing with his father, Christopher Columbus.*

Diego felt a warm glow, despite the foggy chill of morning.

From inside the church, he heard the friars begin their morning prayers. He whispered the familiar words along with them, crouching out of sight. When the service ended, the friars filed out of the church, but still Pinzón had not appeared.

Diego shifted his stiff, cramped legs. "How long must I wait?" he muttered. "Where can he be?"

At last Diego heard footsteps thumping up the path. It sounded like someone big. Pinzón? Or could it be Julio?

Diego stayed down, peering out carefully from his hiding place. He saw a human form emerge from the fog as if by magic. As the person came closer, Diego recognized his bushy beard and confident swagger. It was Pinzón.

Diego leaped to his feet. "Captain, I'm here."

Pinzón jumped. "Who? Who's there?"

"Diego Columbus, sir."

"You could scare a man to death that way, jumping out in a graveyard. You could have been a ghost!"

"I'm no ghost," Diego laughed. "At least not yet, but I *could* be one if I get caught." He gestured toward the church. "I'd feel safer inside."

"What have you done," Pinzón asked, "that you're in hiding?"

"It's a long story," Diego said as they entered the stony cool of the church.

"Tell me first then. Where is your father?"

"I don't know. I was hoping *you'd* tell *me*."

"What's going on here? I got a message: 'Meet me at the church at dawn.' It was signed, 'Columbus.'"

Diego grinned.

"You?" Pinzón growled, stooping to Diego's height. "You sent me that message?"

"I didn't lie. Columbus is my name, too," said Diego. He paused. "Where could he be?"

"Your father? The last time I caught sight of him, we were at sea between here and Palos. A terrible storm was raging and our ships were separated. The *Pínta's* rudder was torn loose. She was set adrift for two full weeks, lost from the rest of the fleet, but we had agreed to meet in the islands if we all survived."

"Why isn't he here then?" Diego demanded.

Pinzón began to pace back and forth. "How should I know? I'm a seaman, not a mystic. He may have gone to Gomera... Who knows? He's probably wondering where *we* are."

"Will you find him? Will you search for him in Gomera?"

"First, I must get the rudder repaired — work that's best done here."

"And then?"

Pinzón frowned. "Sometimes I think this voyage is doomed. Hexed! Perhaps it's not God's will that men should sail so far from land."

"Captain, my father has planned and dreamed — "

"Your father is not a god, you know. He's a mortal, an ordinary man. And just because he wants a thing doesn't mean it *ought* to be. Not when *my* life's at stake." He opened the door of the church. "It looks as though the fog has cleared," he said.

Diego sat alone in the cool quiet of the church.

"Diego," Pinzón cried from the doorway. "Come quick!"

Diego rushed out into the sunshine.

"Look," said Pinzón, pointing out to sea. "The *Santa María*!"

"He's here," Diego exclaimed. "My father is here at last."

"I don't know what *you're* so pleased about. He's going to send you home the minute he sees you."

Eyes sparkling, Diego stroked his chin. "Not if you help me."

"Aha! It looks as though you've got a plan."

Diego grinned. "All I ask is that you send word as soon as it's time to sail. Friar Guillermo will let me stay here until then."

"What will your father say?"

"My father won't know. I'm counting on you not to tell."

Pinzón made a face. "What are you up to, boy?"

"Captain," said Diego, "I plan to be aboard the *Santa María* when she sails."

"Stow away?"

Diego nodded. "My father won't find me until it's too late to turn back."

"That's the craziest thing I've ever heard...Still, it might serve the old boy right."

"You'll help me then?"

"Maybe. Maybe not. I have to think about it."

"You won't tell anyone, will you?"

Pinzón shrugged. "Who would I tell?"

"Good," said Diego. "I must succeed. I *have* to go with him."

"Stubborn, aren't you?" Pinzón laughed. "All right. I promise you one thing — you'll hear from me before the *Pínta* leaves Las Palmas."

"You'll come for me here?"

"Don't push me, boy! I *said* I'll let you know. No more promises. That's it."

"It's enough," Diego said softly. "I can do the rest."

Chapter 20

August 31, 1492

*D*iego scattered bits of leftover bread in the yard beside the church. A mother hen and her chicks clustered around his feet — rustling, pecking, nudging one another.

Friar Guillermo stuck his head out the window. "When you're done, I want you to climb up in the bell tower. We need someone agile to go up there and tighten the ropes."

"I don't know much about bells," Diego warned.

"Never mind. If *you* will climb, then *I* shall stand below and shout. I'll tell you what to do."

Diego tossed the last of the crumbs into the yard. He went into the bell tower and began to climb the narrow stone steps. At the top, he breathed in the smells of age and dust, as if he had climbed — up, down, back — into the past.

"Diego?"

"I'm here," he called, squinting into the musty tower. Ringlets of rope hung from the great greenish bell. "What do you want me to do?"

"Ah! Wait. Someone's coming."

Diego heard a voice from the courtyard. "Hallo, halloo!"

He recognized it in a flash — his father's voice. Christopher Columbus! He'd come here to the church. But why?

"Welcome," Friar Guillermo exclaimed.

Diego lay on his belly and peered through the cracks in the boards, hungry for a glimpse of his father's face. He could see the bronze-red hair, the high cheekbones, and the strong, clean-shaven jaw.

He longed to grab the rope and ring the bell for joy. He wanted to cry out, to rush into his father's arms!

Christopher's voice was calm. "Good evening, Father. I'm Admiral Columbus. I've come for a special reason."

Diego's heart thumped. Did he know?

"What can I do for you?" asked the priest.

Christopher shaded his eyes, gazing toward the sea. "My son, Diego..."

Diego felt hot, burned by sudden fury. *Pinzón told him where to find me! He'll send me back to Palos.*

"Yes?" said Friar Guillermo.

"At this very moment, my son is in a place very like this one. At La Rábida, near Palos. Two places of peace. Both perched high above the sea. They are similar in many ways."

"Strange you should say that," said Friar Guillermo. "There was another person — a young boy — who said the same thing." He stole an upward glance toward the tower.

Diego put his fingers to his lips.

Friar Guillermo winked.

Christopher turned back to face the priest. "So you've heard of La Rábida?"

"A time or two. Your son is there *now*, you say?"

Christopher nodded. "For some reason, I found myself thinking of him as I came up the path."

"Pray for him then."

"Yes, Father, I will. That, in fact, is why I have come. My ships will be sailing in the morning, quite early. Always, before a voyage, I spend some time in prayer, asking the blessing of God before we sail."

Friar Guillermo bowed slightly from the waist. "You are most welcome here." He opened the door of the church and Christopher went inside.

Diego hesitated for a moment, then scrambled down the twisting stairs. Taking Friar Guillermo's hand, Diego pulled him away from the door of the church. "I thought someone had told him I was here," he whispered.

"Ahh! Who would tell him?"

"The only one who knows," Diego said softly. "Pinzón, Captain of the *Pínta*. He promised he'd send for me before he set sail. Pinzón broke his word."

Friar Guillermo rumpled Diego's hair. "You are not very patient, are you, my son? For all we know, the good captain is on his way right now."

"I can't wait any longer. I have to go now!"

"Don't be foolish, boy. You could be seen. Don't forget about Hawk. You've said enough already to keep me wide awake at night." The friar sighed as he spoke.

"There's no time."

"There's always time to be smart."

Diego protested. "If I wait, it'll be dark."

"Come," Friar Guillermo said. "What you need is a good disguise. It won't take long, and then you'll be free to stroll through town while the sun still shines! No one will know."

"A disguise?"

"Of course. A merchant came here not long before he died. A noble man, but short. Surprisingly short! We still have his clothes."

"You want me to dress in a *dead* man's clothes?"

"Better to *dress* like a dead man, son, than risk *becoming* one."

"I can't do that," Diego moaned. "Besides, it wouldn't work. No one would believe that I'm a merchant. I'm only twelve years old!"

"Perhaps you're right..."

Diego closed his eyes. "If only they'd keep away..."

"You want to be invisible," murmured the priest. "Untouchable somehow..."

Diego's eyes opened wide. "That's it. Untouchable! I'll dress like a leper. No one will dare come near me!"

"Perfect," Friar Guillermo declared.

Chapter 21

The Rattle

*D*iego left the church, his body draped in ragged gray cloths. Even his head was hooded in gray. In his hands, he carried a rattle.

"Shake it whenever someone comes near," Friar Guillermo had advised. "The rattle warns the world: I am diseased. Touch *me*, and you'll become a leper, too."

It was dusk when Diego reached the town. The shops had closed, but the streets were still busy. There were fishermen with their catch and children racing home before dark. Whenever Diego shook the rattle, people pulled away. And though he kept his head tucked down, he could see the fear in their faces.

Walking quickly, Diego felt his heart beating double-time. As he neared the harbor, he breathed in the familiar smells of fish and salt seawater. His spirits began to lift.

"Almost there," he whispered.

He could hear men laughing and talking in the ale houses. As he passed the Bull and Anchor, a group of men spilled into the street. Diego stepped back and leaned against the wall. He shook his rattle. One of the men tossed some coins at his feet.

Glancing up, Diego saw that it was Julio. With him were Weasel and Hawk.

Hiding his face, Diego made his voice deep. "Bless you, my brother."

The three walked on.

Diego almost laughed aloud as he gathered up the coins and headed toward the ships.

He saw the *Pínta* and Pinzón, standing alone on the deck.

Diego ran forward.

"Back! Get back," Pinzón cried.

Diego pulled the hood from his head. "It's only me."

"Wretched boy! You frightened me again!"

Diego did not smile. "You *said* you'd let me know before you sailed. Captain, you promised."

"I was going to. I was on my way."

"My father came to the church. He told Friar Guillermo that the fleet sails at dawn."

"That's right. We sail to the island of Gomera."

Diego pounded one fist into the other. "To Gomera first? Why?"

"We'll replenish our supplies there — food, water, and wood — and then we head for the open sea."

"Is there nothing I can count on?" Diego exclaimed. "He keeps changing the plans. All right! He's sailing first to Gomera...Captain, please. I *must* sail to Gomera with you or else, for me, the dream is lost."

"I don't know," said Pinzón, rubbing the bristles of his beard.

"Just until we get to Gomera, Captain! And then I'll stow away on the *Santa María*. You'll never see my face again."

"If I were to let you sail aboard the *Pínta*," Pinzón warned, "you'd have to work — just like all the others."

"I will," Diego promised. "I'll work!"

"Come along then," said Pinzón. "We sail at first light."

Chapter 22

Below Deck

Diego stood on the *Pínta*'s deck, bucket in hand. Las Palmas was behind him. Gomera — and the Indies — lay ahead.

Captain Pinzón appeared. "This is not supposed to be a pleasure trip, young man."

"No, sir," said Diego. "I can't stop smiling though."

"You can't clean a deck by grinning at it."

"I was told to scrub the lower deck. I'm going."

"I thought I made it clear. No special treatment..."

"Don't worry, Captain!" Diego exclaimed. "I'll polish the deck until it shines."

"See that you do," Pinzón snapped.

"When will we get to Gomera?"

"It takes about a day. If we're lucky and if the wind is strong, we should be there by nightfall."

Diego went below. He set the bucket down and knelt beside it.

The sailors were grumbling. "I don't care *who* says not to worry," one of them said. "I've got a family to see to."

"Who *is* this man anyway? Columbus. What does he know? *He's* never sailed out there. No one has, and no one knows what might happen."

"I've heard stories," a third began, "about monsters and storms — all manner of fearsome things."

Pretending not to listen, Diego set to work. Voices tumbled about his head.

"*I* say we band together. Refuse to sail. Why should *he* be free to risk *our* lives, sailing beyond what's known?"

"We have no reason to go. Even if all goes well, he'll get the glory and most of the gold, not us."

"We bear the risk, and I say no."

"The price is too high," a deep voice growled.

"Shhh! That boy — I've never seen him before."

"Hey, you," someone said gruffly.

Humming softly, Diego tipped back on his heels. He pumped his rag up and down in the water, squeezed it out, and began to scrub again.

"Maybe he's not quite right in the head," said another.

"Nahhh, I think he's foreign. Probably can't understand a word we're saying."

Diego said nothing. Just scrubbed.

One of the sailors tapped the bucket with his foot. "Where you from, boy?"

Diego looked up as if surprised.

"I said, where are you from?"

Diego raised his shoulders and shook his head.

"Are you deaf or what?"

For a moment, Diego froze. Then he had an idea. At La Rábida, Friar Pierre had taught him a few words of French. Perhaps it would be enough to get him through.

He smiled. "Je suis francais. Parlez-vous francais?"

The sailors laughed. "Told you he's foreign."

"No need to worry what we say, I guess," said another.

Diego shrugged and set to work again. The sailors went back to their talk.

"*I* say we go no farther than Gomera."

"Mutiny?"

"Call it what you like. First, we must restock the ship for the trip back home."

"Right, and then we take over."

"Aye," said the growly voice. "We take over and sail straight back to Spain."

"Columbus may try to stop us," someone warned.

"If the Admiral has to die at our hands, well then — so be it!"

"Better *his* life than ours."

"Aye. So be it."

Diego kept his back bent, head still. He rubbed the boards of the deck with smooth, regular strokes.

"What about Pinzón?" someone demanded.

"Don't worry about *him*," another voice said calmly. "Leave Pinzón to me."

Diego's breath was coming fast. *Calm . . . stay calm*, he told himself.

"Almost time for our watch," someone said.

As the sailors got to their feet, Diego looked up. Careful to hold his face still — as if it were a mask — he studied the group before him, quickly memorizing each face.

One sailor held up a hand. "Wait," he said. "What we planned . . . no one's to say anything. Not yet."

The others murmured agreement. "Nothing to any- one. Not until closer to time."

Diego watched them leave. "Au revoir," he whis- pered. "Good-bye, but *not* farewell."

September 5, 1492

*T*he setting sun spread a blanket of gold across the
Pínta's deck. For four days, she had lain at anchor at
Gomera in the port town of San Sebastian. From there,
the sailors had gathered food supplies and, traveling
upriver in boats, had cut wood from the inland forests.

Diego had helped to load the ship for the voyage
ahead. Since all the sailors thought he was French, no
one expected him to speak, and no one worried if he
should hear their whispered talk.

Pinzón had only laughed when he heard what Diego
had done. Now the ships were ready to sail.

At the end of his watch, Diego saw Pinzón amid-
ships. No one else was near.

"Do you know where my father is?"

Pinzón laughed. "Your father is . . . *busy*."

"What do you mean — 'busy'?"

Pinzón pointed toward the island. "See that castle?"

Diego nodded.

"The Governor of Gomera lives there. Her name is Doña Beatriz de Peraza."

"A woman? The Governor?"

"That's right. And what a woman she is! More beautiful than any princess in your dreams. Long black hair . . . "

"You've seen her?"

"No, but your father has. And I've heard talk. From all accounts, he's spent quite a lot of time in that castle. And who could blame him? He's there now, having dinner with the lady. Bidding her a fond farewell, I should think."

Diego scowled.

"What do you care?" Pinzón demanded. "While your father is out of the way, you're free to board the *Santa María*. You can hide until we're well under way. I thought that was your plan."

"It is," said Diego. "It is."

Pinzón tossed a rope ladder across the side of the ship and started down. "I have things to do in town. Alberto will take me ashore, then come for me again in the morning."

"And all three ships will — "

Diego felt a heavy hand across his mouth. Choking, he turned and saw Alberto glaring down at him.

"The little *French* boy, eh?"

"Excusez-moi?" Diego gasped.

"Very funny," Alberto growled. "Very funny."

Diego watched as Alberto and Pinzón climbed down into the rowboat.

When Alberto reached the bottom of the ladder, he looked up. "I'll be back," he said, spitting the words like pebbles from his mouth.

Diego's stomach twisted. Alberto knew! And soon, the others would know. Who would protect him?

There was no one. Even Pinzón was gone.

Nando stood beside the mainsail. Diego saw him beckon to Esequiel and Raul and the three go below deck.

Diego followed them, careful to stay out of sight. Hiding behind a stack of bagged rice, he listened.

"Tomorrow's the day," Nando said hoarsely.

Esequiel chuckled. "We sail, but not to the Indies as planned."

"And a good thing, too," said Nando. "I've heard talk in town. Three Portuguese ships are lying in wait just beyond the islands."

Esequiel shrugged. "So what?"

"The ships are armed, and they're waiting for a certain Spanish fleet — the *Pínta*, the *Niña*, and the *Santa María*."

113

"*Our* ships?" Raul gasped, his pockmarked face growing pale. "They're waiting for *us*? Why?"

"Use your head," Nando snapped. "The Portuguese virtually own the trade route east to the Indies. Do they want a *Spanish* fleet to find a new and better route?"

"I guess not," Raul mumbled. "Do they mean to attack?"

"Sure looks like it."

"Never mind," said Esequiel. "The *Pínta* will be on its way to Spain by then. Admiral Columbus will have to manage with two ships. Let *him* face the Portuguese guns."

"What about Pinzón?" Raul asked.

Nando's voice was stern. "I told you once. Forget Pinzón. I've decided to leave him just where he is — out of the way, in San Sebastian. We don't need him anyway. From now on, *I* give the commands. Everyone takes orders from *me*. Understand?"

The others murmured consent.

"Tomorrow, just before dawn, we'll gather the crew of the *Pínta*. With both Pinzón and Columbus gone, the men will do whatever we say. They'll have no choice."

Diego waited until the group split up, then ran to the upper deck. He looked toward San Sebastian, and though it was getting dark, he could see the rowboat in the distance — and Alberto pushing off from shore, heading back to the ship.

Diego climbed over the rail and scrambled down the ladder. Gasping as his body slid into the water, he began to swim. With every stroke he made, the rowboat grew larger. He could see the back of Alberto's dark blue shirt as he pulled the oars toward him.

When Diego could almost touch the boat, he took a deep breath, dived down, and swam underwater. He could hear the echo of the oars, dipping and pulling, above his head.

When he surfaced, the sky was almost black, but the rowboat was gone. Panting, he swam on.

At last his feet scraped bottom, and Diego stumbled ashore. Dripping and shivering, he stopped a fisherman.

"Which way to the castle?" he asked.

"Fine time to make a call!"

"Please," Diego gasped. "Just tell me."

The fisherman shrugged. "Go along the shore. When you get to the forest, you'll see the castle road. Just walk through the woods and you'll see it."

"Through the woods?" Diego breathed. "Through the dark?"

"It's the only way to get there."

Chapter *24*

Beyond the Dark

"*J*ust warn him," Diego panted, sprinting along the shore. "Tell Father. About Nando."

As the shoreline receded, the forest loomed ahead. Diego saw the castle road leading into the woods. There, darkness yawned like the mouth of a cave.

He slowed his pace, fighting the urge to turn back. He could find safety somewhere, somehow in town...

"No," Diego said aloud. He stuffed his hands in his pockets and kept going.

As the trees closed over his head, he could see faint patterns traced by the moon on the path. The forest itself seemed to be alive, rustling and whispering at every turn. Shining eyes flickered among the trees. Was it a wolf or a robber who hid there, waiting?

Once again, his fears took shape and perched along the path. They hid in the trees and hooted from the shadows. They sat on the tops of rocks, like toads with bulging eyes and darting tongues.

Diego's heart pounded. His face burned and his knees trembled. Suddenly, he was five years old again. His mother was dead, and he was lost, all alone, in the forest.

"God help me," he whispered, blinking back tears. "For the sake of the dream, God help!"

Diego took a deep breath and began to sing as he walked. The music that came to his lips was a song Friar Pierre used to chant as he worked in the garden at La Rábida. Diego pretended that the priest was walking beside him and the two of them sang it together:

> *Eternal light, shine in my heart.*
> *Eternal hope, lift up my eyes.*
> *Eternal wisdom, make me wise.*
> *Eternal brightness, help me see.*

Whenever Nando's face swam into Diego's mind, he chased it away with song. And at last the trees gave way to open sky.

Seeing the moon and stars again, Diego laughed aloud. "I did it," he cried. "I did it!"

Before him stretched a hill and perched on top was a castle built of stone. Diego ran toward it.

As he reached the gate, a guard called out, "Who goes there?"

"Diego Columbus. I have a message for Admiral Columbus. It's urgent."

"Wait here," said the guard. He turned away.

From the woods came shouts and the thunder of footsteps. Glancing over his shoulder, Diego saw Nando, Alberto, Raul, and Esequiel speeding out of the forest.

"There he is," shouted Raul.

"Take him!" Nando roared as the four men pounded up the path to the castle.

"Halt!" cried the guard. Lifting a horn to his lips, he blew a blast.

From all sides, more guards came running. Diego ducked under the guard's elbow and raced down the corridor. From somewhere in the castle, he heard music. Following that sound, he came to a carved wooden door. Music and light seeped out beneath it.

Breathless, Diego knocked, then pounded. He heard footsteps and the clatter of swords coming toward him.

"Father," he shouted. "Father!"

The door swung open. There stood Christopher Columbus.

"Diego!" the Admiral gasped. He opened his arms and clutched Diego to his chest. "What have you *done*, child?"

Tears rolled, unbidden, down Diego's cheeks. He swiped at them as he tried to explain to his father.

"Men from the ship . . . tried to kill me . . . Followed me here."

"Go back," Christopher shouted to the guards who clattered down the hallway toward them. "The boy is my son. Stop the men who followed him."

"They've been captured, sir. They're in our hands already."

Just then the Governor stepped out. "Well done. Lock them up until we come," she said.

The guards turned back.

Doña Beatriz wrapped her shawl around Diego's shoulders. She led him inside and closed the door. "Poor boy, you're shivering."

"I'm all right," Diego murmured, "now." He turned to his father. "I discovered a mutiny aboard the *Pinta*. That's why Nando and the others wanted my skin!"

Christopher shook his head. "And *I* thought you were tucked away, safe with Friar Juan and Friar Pierre."

Diego touched the cross that hung around his neck. "I was safe, Father. Even in danger — safe! I'll tell you all about it during the voyage."

"The voyage?"

"To the Indies, Father. Let me sail aboard the *Santa María*, please! There'll be no mutiny now, though I must tell you — there's a fleet of Portuguese ships armed and waiting offshore."

"So I've heard," Christopher murmured, "but I'm convinced they're just watching. Making sure we don't sail south toward the Gold Coast."

"You may have known about the ships, but you didn't know about the mutiny."

"I certainly didn't," Christopher said.

Diego's eyes sparkled. "You know what that means, don't you, Father? It means," he rushed on, "that I have saved this voyage once again. I've saved it three times now!"

Doña Beatriz smiled. "It would seem this boy has a *right* to sail with his father."

"He's never been strong. I worry about him on a long voyage."

"*That* again!" Diego laughed. "If only you knew! First I was shipwrecked, and then I was kidnapped in Las Palmas. All sorts of things have happened to me — yet here I am. How can you say that I'm not strong?"

"This boy is *very* like his father," Doña Beatriz laughed. "Look how stubborn he is!"

Diego grinned, then turned again to his father. "Let me go with you," he begged. "Have I not earned a place at your side?"

Christopher Columbus held up his hands. "All right, you win! A new man has just signed on for the voyage."

"Hurrah!" Diego shouted. "Tomorrow, tomorrow we sail to the dream!"

Epilogue

What Do We Know About Diego?

*D*iego Columbus, the real son of Christopher Columbus, was born in 1480 on Porto Santo, an island off the coast of Portugal. He was named after Christopher's younger brother.

When Diego's mother, Doña Felipa, died late in 1484 or early in 1485, Christopher was away from home. Returning home, he took their son, Diego, to live at La Rábida, a monastery near Palos on the coast of southern Spain. Christopher knew the churchmen at La Rábida and had actually lived there for a time himself. He arranged for the friars to take care of Diego while he was traveling from one royal court to another, trying to win support for his voyages.

For Diego, it must have been a terrible time. Having so recently lost his mother, he was forced to say good-bye to his father. Whatever Diego may have thought or said, history tells us that he stayed at La Rábida for almost six years.

We know nothing about Diego's life during that time, but we can be fairly certain that the Franciscan monks at La Rábida fed him well and taught him to read and write. In that way, Diego was ahead of his father, who did not learn to read or write until he was grown.

In the fall of 1491, Christopher came back to La Rábida. He intended to pick up Diego before going to France to try for royal support there. But Friar Juan Perez convinced him to try Spain again and promised to arrange for him to see Queen Isabella.

Despite the Queen's royal welcome, Christopher was turned down again. Fortunately, he had made another powerful friend at court, Luis de Santángel, the royal treasurer. Santángel went to the Queen on the same day that Christopher left the court and convinced her to change her mind.

The Queen sent a messenger for Columbus, who overtook him on the road to Piños-Puente, about ten miles away from the royal court at Granada. Our story, DIEGO COLUMBUS: ADVENTURES ON THE HIGH SEAS, begins here.

Isabella and Ferdinand decreed that the town of Palos must provide two of Christopher's three ships. The order was read aloud to the townspeople and seamen in the parish church of St. George on May 23, 1492. Columbus was there, as was the mayor. The royal order also decreed that civil and criminal charges would be dropped for anyone who signed up for the voyage.

Martín Alonso Pinzón was a town leader in Palos. He went around to the taverns and convinced men to sail with Columbus. Pinzón himself sailed as Captain of the *Pínta*, and many of his relatives joined him on board. In the square of Palos there is, to this day, a statue of Martín Alonso Pinzón. His brother, Vicente Yáñez Pinzón, was Captain of the *Niña*.

Columbus's three ships were amazingly small, compared to oceangoing vessels today. The *Niña*, smallest of the three ships, has been estimated to be around seventy feet long with only one deck. There were about ninety crew members, including ship's boys. The names of eighty-seven men and their wages are recorded. Some of the names appear in Columbus's journal. Some have been retrieved from the Spanish archives because the Crown paid the wages of the crew. According to Columbus's biographer, there were no desertions in the Canaries, although one new hand may have signed on there. Could this sailor have been the Admiral's own son, Diego?

August 3 dawned stifling hot and windless. People said it was the day of the halcyon when the gulls make their nests at sea. And it was a Friday — not a good omen for sailors. Christopher wasn't worried. At dawn he ordered the men to weigh anchor "in the name of Jesus." The crew had to use the oars to go downriver to the ocean. Once in the open sea, they traveled with a good, strong breeze — headed for the Canary Islands and a permanent place in history.

Hunger was not a major fear for those who sailed with Columbus. Enough food, wine, and water were stowed aboard to last a year. Breakfast might well consist of a ship's biscuit (hardtack), some garlic cloves, a bit of cheese, and a pickled sardine. There was one hot meal per day and no bedrooms or dormitories on the small ships. All but the captain were expected to simply lie down and sleep anywhere — on deck in good weather.

One duty of a ship's boy was to watch the *ampolleta* — the hourglass. There were six watches in a day. The ship's boy was to turn the glass every half hour, eight times in a four-hour watch. At each half hour, he was to sing a little song, which changed according to the watch. One such song, shortened a bit and translated, appears in Chapter 8.

Columbus intended to sail first to the Canaries and then on to the Indies. The three ships (the *Pínta*, the *Niña*, and the *Santa María*) would sail together to the Canaries and land on the main island. There they would restock for the second leg of the journey. However, storms separated the small fleet and the rudder on the *Pínta* worked loose.

The *Pínta* limped slowly toward the Grand Canary Island for repairs while the others sailed to Gomera, a less populated island to the west. The *Niña*'s sails had to be changed from triangular sails to square sails which were more suited to the high winds of the open sea. This separation and repairs accounted for the delay in beginning the second part of the voyage.

Though the original plan had been for all three ships to go to Las Palmas, the *Santa María*, with Christopher at its helm, landed at the small port of San Sebastian on August 12, 1492. He did not go to Las Palmas for almost two weeks. He was waiting for the return of the island's beautiful young governor, Doña Beatriz de Peraza. Meanwhile, Martín Alonso Pinzón was busy in Las Palmas, trying to get the *Pinta* repaired.

On August 25, Pinzón and Columbus met in Las Palmas and revised their plans. On September 1, all three ships left Las Palmas, arriving at Gomera on September 2. At last Columbus had all three ships in one port.

Columbus was full of confidence as he looked toward the voyage, but the men were afraid. Most had been uneasy from the start. Given the men's fears, it is surprising that no one deserted in the Canaries. But that doesn't mean they stopped worrying and wishing for home. They worried that if they sailed around the surface of the earth, they might not be able to sail back home. They were not worried that they would fall off the edge of the earth. People had long realized that the earth was round.

Columbus was a powerful, persuasive man, but he would need someone to warn him if the men's fears were getting out of hand. He needed a spy. Who better than the Admiral's own son to warn him of mutiny?

On September 9, the fleet of three ships left the Canaries. Columbus was warned that three Portuguese ships were cruising just beyond Gomera, possibly intending to attack his fleet. Those ships were never spotted. By nighttime, all sight of land was gone. The *Pínta*, the *Niña*, and the *Santa María* were sailing into uncharted seas.

Because he understood the fears of his crew, Christopher tried to keep them from panic. One method he used was a trick. He kept two separate logs (travel records). His private journal recorded his true estimate of the miles traveled; the other showed fewer miles for each day of the journey. Perhaps this helped, but after a month, the men's fears were leading them close to mutiny. Almost everyone wanted to turn back. There was whispered talk that their problems would be solved if Christopher were to *accidentally* fall overboard and drown! On October 10, 1492, Columbus was forced to compromise. He promised that if land were not sighted in two or three days, he would turn back.

On October 12, 1492, at 2:00 A.M., land was sighted. Everyone wept and sang for joy. When the ships were anchored, Christopher and the other officers rowed ashore. Did a proud Diego splash onto the beach as his father claimed the island in the name of Spain?

Historical records from this time vary a great deal. There were no newspapers, no computers, no tape recorders, and no bank vaults for safekeeping valuable papers. Often the original letter or document has been lost, and all that we have are handwritten copies. Was anything changed or left out?

In studying the papers that do come to us across the years, historians must ask: Who was writing and why? Did the writer see what is described, or did he hear about it from someone else? Was it written at the time it happened or many years later, after memory had begun to cloud?

Though the historical records tell us very little about Diego after 1491, we know for certain that in 1509 he sailed across the ocean to Santo Domingo, an island that Christopher Columbus had named after his own father — Diego's grandfather. We also know of a letter that Christopher wrote to Diego in 1502 before his fourth and final voyage. A rare, handwritten copy of this letter has recently been discovered. In it, Christopher speaks of the love that he and Diego have for each other. History tells us that Diego remained close to his father and was at Christopher's bedside when the great explorer died in 1506.